PENGUIN CANADA

FRIENDSHIPS

BUDGE WILSON was born in Halifax, Nova Scotia, and attended Dalhousie University and the University of Toronto. Since 1984, she has published twenty-nine books, with twenty foreign editions appearing in the United States, Norway, Sweden, Finland, Denmark, Romania, Germany, Italy, Greece, and Australia. Her stories appear in ninety anthologies, in Braille format, and as audiobooks. Her many prizes include nineteen Canadian Children's Book Centre "Our Choice" awards, the City of Dartmouth Book Award, the Canadian Library Association's Young Adult Canadian Book Award, the Marianna Dempster Award, the Ann Connor Brimer Award, the Lilla Stirling Award, and first prize (adult fiction) in the CBC Literary Competition. Her collection of short stories *The Leaving* was named a Notable Book by the American Library Association and was later included on the association's list of "The 75 Best Children's Books of the Last 25 Years." Wilson has also been awarded the Municipality of Halifax Mayor's Award for Cultural Achievement in Literature and received the Distinguished Alumni Award from Armbrae Academy, Halifax. In 2004, she was made a Member of the Order of Canada.

Also by Budge Wilson (selected titles)

friendships

stories

budge wilson

PENGUIN
CANADA

PENGUIN CANADA

Published by the Penguin Group

Penguin Group (Canada), 90 Eglinton Avenue East, Suite 700, Toronto, Ontario, Canada
M4P 2Y3 (a division of Pearson Penguin Canada Inc.)

Penguin Group (USA) Inc., 375 Hudson Street, New York, New York 10014, U.S.A.
Penguin Books Ltd, 80 Strand, London WC2R 0RL, England
Penguin Ireland, 25 St Stephen's Green, Dublin 2, Ireland (a division of Penguin Books Ltd)
Penguin Group (Australia), 250 Camberwell Road, Camberwell, Victoria 3124, Australia
(a division of Pearson Australia Group Pty Ltd)
Penguin Books India Pvt Ltd, 11 Community Centre, Panchsheel Park, New Delhi – 110 017,
India
Penguin Group (NZ), cnr Airborne and Rosedale Roads, Albany, Auckland 1310, New Zealand
(a division of Pearson New Zealand Ltd)
Penguin Books (South Africa) (Pty) Ltd, 24 Sturdee Avenue, Rosebank, Johannesburg 2196,
South Africa

Penguin Books Ltd, Registered Offices: 80 Strand, London WC2R 0RL, England

First published 2006

1 2 3 4 5 6 7 8 9 10 (WEB)

LIBRARY AND ARCHIVES CANADA CATALOGUING IN PUBLICATION

Wilson, Budge
Friendships / Budge Wilson.

ISBN 0-14-301766-7

1. Children's stories, Canadian (English). I. Title.

PS8595.I5813F75   2006   jC813'.54   C2005-906807-8

Visit the Penguin Group (Canada) website at **www.penguin.ca**

Special and corporate bulk purchase rates available;
please see **www.penguin.ca/corporatesales** or call 1-800-399-6858, ext. 477 or 474.

This book is for
my friend
Marjie Wilde

A friend may well be reckoned
the masterpiece of nature.
—RALPH WALDO EMERSON

contents

introduction

S ometimes it's hard to recognize a friend, nor is a friend always a person. A friend can be an animal or a thought or a way of looking at things. Friendships can be between very diverse people—of differing ages, lifestyles, sexes, races, and social classes. But a friend is someone you like, someone you want to spend time with or think about. Without that friend, you'd be less comfortable in your life, less *safe*. A friend is someone who listens to you when you talk, and who understands what you're saying.

All the stories in this book are about friendships. Sometimes they are unusual ones. One story is about two people who become friends before they've even met. One brother can be a friend, another an enemy. Even a parent can turn into a friend if a door of communication opens up between the two people. In a good friendship there is a lot of trust, based on a mutual confidence that is often difficult to define.

A dependable friend can help you get through very troubling times, and will support you until you come out on the other side of your problem. Disloyal friends can break your heart. If they do that, they are no longer friends. They are something else.

You may think that in some of these stories there is no friend. Think again. You could be wrong. "The Snake" may leave you guessing. And who on earth is the friend in "Lillian"? If you are looking for a collection of short stories in which each one is about a peer friendship, you're looking in the wrong book. It's up to you to figure out who the friends are.

The Snake

Here she was in this place—in this place where she didn't want to be. She was sitting on a granite boulder, smoking a cigarette. Secretly, she hated cigarettes, but smoking one right now gave her a satisfying sense of control and defiance. Being only fifteen years old, she was also breaking the law, which she felt to be an extra bonus. She was taking her legitimate twenty-minute break from her position as a CIT—a counsellor in training—at Camp Wapasat. This role was supposed to provide her with the know-how and the necessary certificate for future jobs within the summer camp system. The sound she was now making was a cross between a cough and a snort, but it was really a short, ironic laugh. As though she would ever even *consider* a job as counsellor within the summer camp system! Starving to death would be infinitely preferable to any such move.

Kate raised her head and tossed her spent cigarette—the butt—into the lake. The lake was so calm and so clear that the butt created a succession of concentric circles on the surface, reaching out and out, around and around, until they were swallowed up by the stillness. On the rocky point, a heron was fishing, standing motionless, waiting for some sign that it was time to attack his prey. A perfect mirror image of him stood upside down on the foreground water. A loon emerged from behind the small island to Kate's left, swimming purposefully to the right. Loons don't just sit around the way ducks and gulls sometimes like to do. A loon is always on the move. All this would seem very beautiful to anyone lucky enough to see it. Kate saw nothing. She was deep inside her own head, focused on the images and the thoughts that inhabited her brain. There was no room in there for loons or herons or still waters.

What was inside Kate's head could be broken down into three categories, and each category was deeply imbedded in anxiety. The three categories were: Campers; Snakes; Time.

Campers. They were all eleven and twelve years old, and all girls. Everyone knows that this is the most dangerous age for girls. They are neither kids nor teenagers. They can be on the brink of puberty, or hotly in the middle of it. As a result, they're uneasy about both worlds, and scared shitless of the one they're in. Through some obtuse psychological absence of logic, this makes most of them appear overconfident and defiant, smug and conceited. These are the ones who are secretive and often devious in their relationships. The rest of them are silent with apprehension; this can make them sheep, willing to be led almost anywhere, by anyone who looks like a leader.

Nellie McGuire had decided she was a leader, and everyone believed her—including Kate. Nellie lived in cabin number seven—Kate's lucky number until one week ago—with four other campers. The sixth bed was occupied by Kate, who was supposed to both inspire them and keep them in line. It took Nellie McGuire only half a day to convince the other four girls that Kate was incapable of either inspiration or discipline. This gave the entire cabin a welcome sense of power and the willingness to use it. Kate was the victim, and the weapon was fear.

But possibly "the entire cabin" is not quite accurate. Collette Jodrey was eleven years old, thin, red haired, and prone to savage sunburns. She liked Kate, and was opposed to the conspiracy to destroy her. But her awe of Nellie was stronger than her sympathy for Kate. If Nellie could be this cruel to a CIT, what might she not do to the shyest girl in the cabin? The possibilities were limitless.

But for Kate, there weren't just possibilities. There were realities. The kids giggled and shrieked after lights out. They refused to make up their bunks, and number seven had the lowest mark in the camp for cabin tidiness. When it was time for swimming hour, and Kate asked them to *walk* on the dock, they raced around as though demented, pushing one another off the edge. Collette was terrified, and so was Kate. She knew she could save one child from drowning, and possibly two. She couldn't save all five simultaneously. When she yelled at them to return to the wharf for their swimming lesson, Nellie shrieked with laughter. The others followed suit, even Collette Jodrey.

So, as Kate sat on her rock, staring at the lake she couldn't see, she thought about how scared she was of the campers. And this was linked to her second big terror—her fear of snakes. She knew that if Nellie McGuire put a snake in her boot, her backpack, her *bed*, they would have to call 911 and bring in an ambulance to carry Kate away to an intensive care unit. Or directly to the Nova Scotia Hospital, which everyone knows is the provincial mental hospital. After all, Nellie had already put a June bug in Collette's drinking glass. It could happen.

Most people are aware that there are no poisonous snakes in Nova Scotia. Maybe that should have made Kate happy, but it didn't. The way they slithered noiselessly among the grasses, the sight of that low and rapid movement—so quick that it was over almost as soon as it happened—caused Kate to feel physically sick. The sight of their coiled-up bodies— cold, slimy—curled on a flat rock, their tiny tongues thrusting in and out, made her weak with an unreasonable horror. She imagined reaching into her backpack for her flashlight and feeling a slippery, writhing body. At that thought, Kate came close to losing her breakfast.

And the third anxiety? Perhaps it wasn't exactly a fear. It was a helpless feeling that maybe she'd be unable to endure five more weeks of this existence. She'd lived through one week without fainting or screaming or attacking Nellie McGuire with her bare hands. Or running into the woods as a grim alternative. Even getting through a day was hard. But five more *weeks*? Yes. *Time* really *was* the third thing Kate was afraid of.

But now she had to return to the battlefield. She tried to walk with confidence, to stride purposefully. But anyone talented at reading body language could have told you that Kate's eyes were wary, her gait not entirely steady. Her first assignment this afternoon was to be a session on Nature. This title covered a lot of territory—pollution, plants, wildlife of all kinds, environmental concerns. Back at the camp, while collecting her notes, she avoided thinking about that cigarette butt and its concentric circles.

The kids seemed almost co-operative as they took the long path down to the beach. She led them along the shore, investigating tidal pools, discussing algae, talking about life cycles, seasonal aberrations. She did witness Nellie casting her eyes to the heavens and muttering. "Boring! *BO-RING!*" But the accompanying titters were subdued, and Kate didn't freeze up and refuse to go on. As they walked along the beach, several of them asked questions, and she was able to answer most of them. This was going along better than she'd dared hope.

"What about snakes?" Nellie's voice broke one of their silences.

There was a pause of maybe three seconds. "What about them?" countered Kate.

"Well, everybody's scared of them. How come?" Nellie was watching Kate very closely.

Kate had anticipated something like this, so she was careful. "As you may know," she began, "none of the snakes in Nova Scotia are poisonous. So there's really nothing to be afraid of. Most of them have beautiful patterns on their backs. Sometimes— periodically, in fact—they shed their skins. Their little tongues are harmless—kind of cute, in fact." Kate took a deep breath. Couldn't someone ask another question? Couldn't they hurry up and get off the subject of snakes?

Fortunately, Nellie ran on ahead, through a field, with Evelyn, her closest sidekick. Everyone had brought along lightweight containers—cast-offs from Dairy Queen, white plastic buckets with handles— into which they dropped specimens that interested them—some blueberries, an odd-shaped leaf, a sand dollar from the beach, a sprig of dusty miller. Kate could see Nellie breaking off bits of fern and spruce and placing them in her bucket. Back at the camp, they'd identify things and maybe set up a display. Kate felt almost content. Things were going well. Maybe Nellie had passed through a phase and left it behind. She watched as the two girls leaned down and pointed to a specimen, obviously discussing it. Kate could feel a little spindle of hope—almost of pride—vibrating weakly in her chest.

Over to the left, one of the campers yelled, "Hey! Wait'll you see what I found! The biggest ladybug in the world!" A couple of girls rushed over to see it, and there were murmurs of admiration. Then they returned to their own searches.

Another girl cried out, "Kate! What's a big crab shell doing up on these dunes? The tide doesn't come up here."

"A gull probably dropped it," shouted Kate, grateful that she could supply an answer that might be right.

It was almost time to head back to the camp. Kate called the campers and asked them to gather together before starting the long trek back to the lake and cabins. The girls were smiling as they approached her, and she smiled back.

"We've brought you a little present," said Evelyn as they came closer. "Something you'll really like."

Kate felt her chest warming. Could this really be happening? It was almost too good to be true.

When Nellie reached the rest of the group, she placed her bucket on the ground. "We knew you'd love it," she said, "so Evelyn put it in my bucket for you."

Kate could feel a physical jolt in her chest, just below her collarbone. Those smiles were too fixed, too cold. She knew what she'd find in that bucket, entwined around the ferns, slithering among the blueberries. She faced the two girls, her smile as fixed as theirs, her eyes as cold.

She was surprised by the steadiness of her voice. "Good!" she said, as she leaned over to look at the snake, her body weak with nausea. "A lovely snake! And a good size, too. Look at the beautiful pattern on his skin, his tiny face. Just like I told you." She turned to the other girls. "Take a good look, kids, before we let him go. It's a great chance to see one up close." She held on tightly to the sides of the bucket so that no one would see her hands shaking.

Nellie looked hard at Kate. "You're right," she said, smiling, smiling. "He's a beautiful specimen. But he's hard to see among all those ferns and leaves and stuff. Pick him up, Kate, and let us *really* see him."

Kate's heart was pumping so hard that it felt as though it might break through her chest wall. But her smile remained. There must be some way she could escape from this. An urgent call to the toilet. A coughing fit. A sudden recollection of something she needed to do back at the camp. Still smiling, she looked around at the girls now standing in a semi-circle in front of her. All of them except Collette—who was carefully studying the toe of her sneaker—were watching her, faces serious now, eyes steady.

No. There was clearly no escape. Kate took a deep breath, to steady herself. Then she bent down and pulled the ferns and large leaves out of the bucket. She had to at least be able to see what she was doing. Then she put her hand into the pail and placed her fingers around the snake, about four inches from his head.

Later on, she often tried to describe what happened at that moment and in the minutes that followed, but she was unable to communicate—even

to herself—the details or pattern of her experience
or its magnitude.

When her hand closed around the snake's body,
her first sensation was of warmth. Off on the edge of
her mind somewhere was also the realization that the
snake wasn't slimy, wasn't wet, wasn't slippery. But it
was the warmth that struck her most forcefully. With
the sensation of warmth came the realization—deep
and knowing—that this was *a living thing*. Of course
she had always known that snakes were alive. It would
be dumb to say otherwise. But this was a different
kind of knowledge. She felt a kinship with it, a
sharing of something. It moved, but it didn't struggle
or writhe. Its little face looked at her, and the little
pink tongue came and went. It was like a light-
hearted conversation.

Kate dropped to her knees and lifted him out of
the bucket (he was a he now, instead of an it, but
not—for some obscure reason—a she). Holding him
so that he faced her, she spoke to him. "Don't be
frightened, little guy," she said. "We'll set you free in
a few moments. We're just here to say hello." She held

him with both hands now, wondering at the feel of his small, strong muscles, the *sturdiness* of him. She felt like crying, and she knew that it was joy that was making her feel this way. She knew, without thinking about it, that the little snake was giving her something that she'd never possessed before.

Turning to the girls, her face alive with the pleasure of what she was feeling, she held him out, and said, "Here. Does anyone else want to hold him? It's a lovely sensation." Then she added, "I'm calling him Charlie."

There was a chorus of noes. Nellie actually stepped back two paces and wrapped her arms around her chest.

"Evelyn?" said Kate. "You've already picked him up. So you know what it's like."

"No," said Evelyn. "I picked him up with the tongs you gave us for handling some of our specimens. I didn't touch him. No."

Kate fought back the desire to say, Nyah! Nyah! Nyah! to them—or the equivalent.

"That's okay," she said. "Maybe some other time. Anyone else?"

Collette watched Kate and the snake with something like envy and spoke slowly: "If you keep holding him, I'd sort of like to just touch him."

She came forward shyly, and reached out to feel the snake's back with the tip of her index finger. Then, with the flat of her hand. Finally, she curled her fingers around the snake's body, feeling his warmth, feeling his muscular movements. She and Kate looked at each other and smiled. Then, without even conferring about it, they opened their hands and set the snake free.

On the way back to camp, the group was very quiet. No one mentioned the snake. No one whispered or tittered. Collette walked tall, her eyes focused and firm, a smile on her lips.

Before they left the field, Kate looked back at the waving grasses, the sand dunes, the glimpse of the sea beyond them. She entered the woods, marvelling at the density of the trees, the birdsong all around them, faint rustling sounds in the low bushes, the sun filtering through the branches. She'd already been at this camp for seven days. How was it that she'd never noticed these things before?

Oh well, she still had five weeks in which to enjoy them. And around the next turn would be their first view of the lake. In half an hour, it would be time for her to supervise her group as they got ready for their swimming lesson. She knew, and did not know how she knew, that it would all go well.

She stopped on the path for a moment and looked up at the tips of the trees as they touched the sky.

"Thank you, Charlie," she whispered.

Bruno

Bullies are big news these days. Everyone knows that. Just walk in the front door of any school. Maybe there'll be a notice board with a small sign that says:

> Parents meeting tonight
> Speech by local psychiatrist
> "Understanding
> Today's Bully"

or perhaps there's a humongous poster beside the principal's office that asks:

WERE YOU A BULLY THIS WEEK?

I know about these signs because I used to be on the school basketball team, and got to go to a lot of other schools. The one that breaks me up is everywhere you look. It's "How can you recognize a bully?" What a laugh. If they're cruel at home, the parents are too ashamed to tell anybody. Or maybe their parents don't know. Those kinds of bullies are often so busy being helpful and polite and kind at home that no one in the family knows who they really are. Or perhaps they're just silent and careful. But never mean. Same with teachers. Bullies really know how to put blinkers on the eyes of a teacher. *Yes sir, no sir. Certainly, Mrs. Homewood; I'll do it right away. Smile, smile. Wide-open eyes. Innocent as the dawn.*

But ask any kid. *They* know who the bullies are, and also where to find them. You find them where the victims are. And the victims are easy to locate. They're the ones who are skinny and short and probably uncoordinated. They trip over things, and they have a scared look. It's the scared look that gives them away. Bullies salivate in the presence of victims, especially when they spot a limp or a flock of pimples or an extra-thick pair of glasses or a stutter. If the scared look is added, they move in for the kill. Bullies want to win—every single time. They know they can push those kids around without getting pushed back.

But there's another class of victim that captures a bully's attention. This group contains kids who are popular, athletic, oppressively handsome or beautiful. Bullies want to either *possess* those people or knock them down to size. Either route will do fine. If the class president is your best friend, you win without even trying. But it can be even more fun to make him look small, to make him look like someone who doesn't deserve all that praise and honour. Keep your eyes open. You'll see those bullies either snuggling up to the school heroes or else sticking pins in them when they're not around. Girls are particularly talented at this form of bullying. Given my choice, I'd prefer a boy and a straight punch in the gut.

It's not hard to see that I'm an authority on bullies. That's because my brother is a bully, and has been one ever since I can remember. His name is Bruno. He was born first. He had golden hair and curls and a turned-up nose. Everyone thought he was the most adorable child in the city, and told him so—everybody except our father, who was jealous of all the attention he was getting and the way his wife was so busy worshipping her son that she didn't seem to know her husband was alive any more. He also thought Bruno's curls made him look like a girl. This bugged him so much that he cut them off one day when my mother was out getting groceries. That was when Bruno was about three and a half, and knew that he was the most beautiful and most loved child in the world, and strutted around as if he was thinking, *Everyone knows I'm adorable, and so do I.* But the result of the haircut was that now he looked more like a pig than a lovable little boy. When my mother came home, she was so shocked and grief-stricken that she went into premature labour and gave birth to me an hour later in the IWK Hospital on University Avenue.

Our next-door neighbour Mrs. Hilton came to look after Bruno while my father rushed my mother to the hospital. She swept up the curls and never once told Bruno that he was cute. My mother left the house screaming, whether from labour pains or rage and sorrow nobody knew or nobody told.

Mrs. Hilton informed me of all these things when I was twelve and had started looking after her garden for three dollars an hour. She was getting old and found it hard to bend over. She also hated Bruno, who was then almost sixteen. Over the years, he had stomped on her flowers, kicked her dog, pulled her cat's tail, and broken at least two of her windows. Maybe he blamed her for me being born. My arrival was certainly the absolute end of his adorable period.

My father didn't like Bruno any better when he looked like a pig than when he looked like an angel. Mothers usually go on loving their children no matter how they look or what they do; but Mrs. Hilton told me that Mom sort of cooled off on Bruno now that he was no longer the most cherubic child in Halifax. Besides, she had this new baby to look after. I was two months premature, and had colic. I cried for nineteen hours out of twenty-four. Her milk dried up, so she had to spend half her life sterilizing bottles. She had no time for Bruno. She got almost no sleep. It was four and a half months before I smiled. No one was smiling at Bruno.

Mrs. Hilton would come over and watch the performance. But Bruno had kicked her in the shins so many times that there wasn't any way she was going to offer to take him off Mom's hands for a few hours.

Mrs. Hilton was sort of the biographer of our family. After I'd weeded her garden and tied up her tomato plants and sprayed her roses for one summer, there was very little I didn't know about my family. She told me that my mom never quite got over being mad at Dad for turning Bruno from an angel into a pig. He had almost *shaved* Bruno's head. It was that close. When his hair grew back, the curls were gone and so was the golden colour. He just looked like any old ordinary boy, with brown hair, a kind of smushed-in-looking nose, and a perpetual frown. What was there to smile about?

My dad stayed away from home a lot because he couldn't stand all the crying. There certainly was nothing about the new baby—me, Westin—to make him jealous. I was shrunken and puny-looking, and the only thing I did well was cry. Colic is supposed to be painful, so I guess I cried from pain and hunger, and from all the times Bruno pinched my leg. My dad—probably racked with guilt and jangling nerves—would smack Bruno when he did that, and then Mom would look at Dad with so much hate that it didn't require any words to communicate to him what she was thinking.

Mrs. Hilton did me a big service, because she helped me understand why Bruno grew up to be so awful. But I was twelve years old before I learned all that, and I wouldn't even have learned it then, if Mrs. Hilton hadn't had such a big mouth. However, twelve is a lot of years to be scared of your bully of a brother, and to have a mother who was—although probably loving—chilly and sad. No hugs in our family. Just shelter and food, which of course a lot of kids would be wildly delighted to have. But when you are five years old or eight or ten, you don't think about those other kids.

When I was five, I started primary. It was a P-to-3 school, so Bruno was in the same building. There were other bullies in the school, but he was the one I feared the most. I'd already had five years of his punches and insults ("You look like a toad"; "You waddle like a walrus"; "Nobody likes you")—enough to pretty well strip me of every milligram of self-confidence. I was overweight from comfort eating, and I already wore glasses. He lay in wait in the halls, whispered behind his hand to his friends, and joined them in their wild derisive laughter. He told the other kids in kindergarten that I was a nerd. They were old enough to know what a nerd was, and they believed him.

One day Bruno stationed himself in the middle of the jungle gym and yelled, "My brother, Westin, wets his pants every night!" It wasn't true. But that night I did. My father spanked my wet bottom and told me he was ashamed of me. I don't need to tell you that I became a chronic bedwetter.

One day I made the mistake of complaining to my mother that Bruno was pulling down my Lego constructions and tearing up my drawings. She told my father.

"Don't be such a wimp, Westin," he growled. "Stick up for yourself. Be a man." (I was six at the time.) "He's not worth bothering about. He's a triple pain in the ass. Give it to him." But I was too little and too scared to follow through on his advice.

Bruno heard all that. He punched me in the face so hard that I didn't go back to school for four days. My mother didn't know how to explain all those bruises to the teacher. Or to anyone else, for that matter. She kept me inside, in my room.

By the time I was in Grade 5, I'd lost all that early fat, and I could run like a cheetah—which just happens to be the fastest animal in the world. Maybe I got that way from being chased by Bruno. I was neurotic, but I was both smart and athletic. That year, I laboriously prepared a project for the science fair. It was a tiny replica of a power dam, with all its components constructed with accuracy and loving care. The teacher told me that I would almost certainly win.

On the evening before the fair, Bruno got up on a chair and jumped down on my project, smashing the little water wheels, the miniature dam, the intricately constructed powerhouse. That night I experienced the depth of pain that a broken heart can reach.

My father came in just after the devastating jump. He had wanted me to win. He'd never won anything in his life, and I think he thought that some of my glory would rub off on him. He wasn't jealous of me the way he had been of Bruno when he was the most beautiful baby in Halifax. He was beginning to want something to be proud of. He was starting to like my high marks and the way I could win ribbons on track-and-field day.

He picked up Bruno by his arm and took him out to the garage. He beat him with an old belt until they must have heard his screams in Point Pleasant Park. Bruno didn't blame Dad for that beating. He blamed me. And never let me forget it.

My mother tried to comfort me, but she didn't know how to do it. She said, "I'm sorry, Westin. I wish he was different." Then she shrugged. "I've tried everything. Nothing works." She was starting to get complaints from teachers and from other parents. She sighed. "He used to be such a darling little boy."

It was beyond my powers of imagination to think of Bruno as a darling little boy. But by the time I was fifteen and had been working on Mrs. Hilton's garden for three summers, I was moving out of my victim status. She had told me so many stories about my family that I was starting to know who I was. And better still, she had a willing and eager ear for any tales I might need to tell about Bruno. For me, she was a combination information centre and safety valve. I didn't fight back when Bruno punched me; he was five inches taller than I was, and had muscles of steel. I'd just spit on the floor and leave the room. And I didn't know how to deal with the white-hot rage that he seemed to carry around with him like a deadly laser beam. So I just kept out of his way and let him polish his reputation as the school's most feared bully. Besides, at the end of June, he'd be either graduating from St. Pat's or else dropping out. He was hanging around with a biker gang, and it was easy to see that he was itching to get on those wheels. You could tell that the members were looking him over. He was tough enough, and didn't seem to have any inconvenient morals that would get in the way of illegal things they might want to do. But he had no bike. That was his big aim that year. He was piling up money in his bank account, and it wasn't hard to figure out where it was coming from.

My own big ambition was to get on the school's basketball team. I was only fifteen and of medium height. But I was thin, wiry, and very fast. I had coordination to die for, and I could jump higher than people who were four inches taller than I was. It could happen. All my fingers and toes were crossed. I felt like a girl doing it, but on the night before they chose the team, I made my wish on the first star:

> Star light, star bright,
> The first star I've seen tonight,
> I wish I may, I wish I might
> Have the wish I wish tonight.

I made the team. They gave me a uniform with a number. I'd have my picture in the yearbook. If we won games, they'd mention it on Information Morning. My father was pleased. Stiffly, he patted me on the back. My mother smiled proudly and squeezed my arm. It was as though all the suns in the universe had come down to shine upon me.

When he heard us talking about it, Bruno left the kitchen by the back porch, slamming the door behind him. I didn't care. Nothing could spoil this. *Nothing*.

I went off to school the next day feeling like a brand-new person. In fact, I think I was. Everything looked different—the blazing autumn leaves had a neon quality for me. The sidewalk was like the Yellow Brick Road. The cars on Windsor Street seemed shinier, faster. I felt as if I was walking to music. There was a basketball practice that afternoon. I knew I'd be able to jump higher than I'd ever jumped before. That's because I had wings.

Mrs. Hilton came to all the games that were played in Halifax. Bruno said that was because she was old and had nothing better to do. I didn't care what he said. I waved to her at halftime.

For the first time in my life, I was part of a group that really cared about one another. We came first in the Regionals and moved on to compete in the Provincials, playing thirteen games that winter, and losing only two. It was suddenly clear to me that we might become provincial champions. It was possible. We could win the banner, and it would hang in the gym forever, reminding me of a whole lot of things. I could come back to the gym and look at it when I became an old man of forty. I went to bed each night dreaming of it. Dreaming of it when I was awake; dreaming of it when asleep.

On the evening before the final championship game, I was waiting to hear from my girlfriend, Stella, who had said she'd phone me to wish me luck. The game was to be in Truro. Bruno yelled up the stairs that there was a call for me. I hadn't heard the phone ring. I dashed out of my room and started to race down the stairs. On the fourth step, there was a pile of books in the dead centre of it.

When I woke up, I was in the hospital and it was the next day. I had a plaster cast on each leg and thirteen stitches in my forehead. I had a black eye and I was missing one tooth. I had a very big headache, and most of the rest of me hurt. But I knew what hurt most. The big clock on the wall said 10:15. The team had left for Truro an hour ago. I tried to keep my mind on the pain in my legs so that I wouldn't have any room left in my head for that bus. Stella was in the room, and Mom and Dad. I didn't want any of them to see me crying.

It was the end of my basketball career, but it was also the end of Bruno—for me, anyway. When Dad figured out what he'd done—when he found him smiling at my inert body at the bottom of the stairs, and when he read the name inside all the textbooks that were sprinkled around the various steps—he gave him the beating of his life—even though he was eighteen and over six feet tall. The next day, Bruno left for Winnipeg on the back of a motorcycle. He'd have his own bike soon enough. There are ways to get money and get it fast, and I'm sure he knew what they were.

Bruno could have destroyed me—one way or another—before I ever went hurtling down the staircase. It was Mrs. Hilton who saved me—by telling me what she knew about my family. By explaining to me how Bruno got to be Bruno, and how I got to be me. And leading me in the direction of being someone else—even if she didn't know she was doing it.

I'm seventeen now, and I don't play basketball any more. I walk fine, and I can even run. But I'm short, and I can't jump the way I used to. But those team members are still my friends, and Stella and I have a lot of fun together.

Mrs. Hilton died last month. I'm going to plant a little garden in front of her tombstone as soon as the weather warms up a bit. I'll go up once a week and make sure it looks okay. After all, she taught me everything I know about flowers.

Justice

He was a thickset, stocky person, was George, and this, oddly enough, was what drew her to him in the first place. I say oddly enough, because Jill was attracted to tall, lithe men. I should know. I was her best friend and confidante from the time we were in Grade 3. Is there anything I don't know about what she thought and what she did? Not much. She always hung loose, spilled it all out. She didn't want advice. Oh no. She just wanted an open, willing ear that would hear all, understand all, and then shut up about it. And I did all those things. When she told me she punched Harriet Cole in the stomach in Grade 4 because she didn't like the way she chewed gum with her mouth open, I never told a living soul, not even my mother. Especially not my mother. Of course, Harriet told *her* mother, but that's another story entirely. When Jill confessed to me that she'd seen Ian McLeod open his zipper to show her his limp little pink penis, I kept this information to myself. She'd bribed him to do it with nine baseball cards, and he was so excited by the bait that the bulge that had been straining against his jeans moments before collapsed like one of those airless sausage balloons; so she didn't get much after all from those nine baseball cards. When I asked her what made his dick get hard in the first place, she said, "None of your business." Then she changed her mind and said, "I opened my blouse and let him see my bare chest." *Free,* with no exchange of hockey cards or anything else. "Don't tell," she said. I didn't. We were in Grade 8, and this would have been explosive information in those days way back in 1949.

I think if we'd been honest with ourselves, we would have admitted that all of us wished we could be more like Jill. Well then, why couldn't we, why didn't we? But you know as well as I do that those aren't easy questions to answer. Why are some people able to break free and do outrageous things—with no apparent fear of consequences? I'd have been happy enough for Ian McLeod to see my breasts, just as long as he saw them through a keyhole or by standing on a ladder outside my bedroom window. After all, they were bigger and rounder than Jill's. I know that, because we both went to swimming classes at the Y, and between shower and pool, there was always a parade of girls walking to and fro in their altogether.

What I could tell you about women's bodies! You maybe think they're all—the young ones—neat and tidy, with breasts like sturdy little half grapefruits. They're not. Some breasts are built like cones or tubes, some like small soggy pancakes. And the permutations and combinations of nipple shapes would astound you. Some like flat little colourless raisins; some like small round dishes with a pale pink wild strawberry in the centre; some almost brown, with long popped-out centres. And I've seen kids of twelve with masses of cellulite dimpling their fat stomachs.

But much as I wished people knew about the excellence of my breasts, I could never, never have put them on display for Ian McLeod, or anyone else, for that matter. I guess those of us who were reticent about breaking rules—school ones or family ones, and later on, community ones—had an uneasy feeling that Big Brother (or more like it, Big Mother) was always watching us, even if we were alone in a car or on a boat or in the woods—miles and miles from any known human habitation.

But Jill didn't seem to be reticent about anything—about *doing* anything, anyway. Letting the world know about it was another matter. I don't think she told anyone, apart from me, about some of the really awful stuff she did—although the other kids did a lot of guessing.

Her parents thought she was as pure and transparent as the raindrops that fall out of the sky. I had a hard time keeping a straight face, sometimes, when they'd go on and on about her virtues. Tiresome, they were. According to them, she was honest and meticulously trustworthy. She was compassionate

and kind. She was open and communicative. *Honest?*
She lied like a pro, particularly to escape punishment
or to gain admiration. And especially to her mom
and dad. "So what did you do this afternoon, Jill,
sweetie?" "I was doing my homework in the school
library." When what she was really doing was trying
on clothes in Reitman's and stuffing a T-shirt into her
book bag. "And where did you get that cute T-shirt,
sweetheart?" "Brenda gave it to me for helping her
with her math." Brenda being me, and guess who was
helping who with her math?

Compassionate and kind. Oh sure. Like the time
she put the frog in that jittery Gladys Anderson's desk
drawer. When Gladys bent down to get her books
and the thing jumped out right in her *face*, she had
hysterics so badly that they had to take her down to
the school nurse for either a slap or a sedative. Jill
wanted to administer the slap—having heard that a
slap can cure hysterics, and anyway having wanted
to slap Gladys ever since she'd first laid eyes on her.
But Maria Dallas, who really *is* compassionate and
kind, and who plays defence on the basketball team,

intercepted the slap in mid-air, and dragged poor old Gladys off to the nurse's office. Jill, of course, insisted that what she had been about to do was medically sound, which may very well be true.

In high school, all our hormones were popping and sizzling, but for most of us at that time, the only results of all this turbulence were acne and door slamming and furious blushing. Jill had perfect skin, slammed no doors, and was never seen to blush. Why? Because she wasn't holding anything back. While most of the rest of us were hanging on to our virginity for dear life, she was rolling and tumbling on beaches and in the woods and on the back seat of her father's Studebaker—with this one and that one, whoever struck her fancy. She told me about it all when she'd come over to my house, allegedly to study with me. The rest of us felt virtuous and stodgy, boring and frustrated, scornful and envious of those who ignored the rules.

Then George McIsaac moved to Halifax, and everything changed. He was in Grade 11 and so were Jill and I. We were all in the same homeroom, so I was able to witness the unfolding drama every day of my life.

We never understood what made George so attractive to all of us. He wasn't handsome in the usual accepted definition of the term. He had kind of a big broad nose and a wide mouth with what Jill called "a wicked grin." But it wasn't wicked. To me, it was a shot of warmth on a chilly day, a flash of light in a dark attic. And his eyes were deep blue and expressive of whatever he was feeling—delight, scorn, anger. He wasn't tall, but he had a powerful body from football, from hockey, from weightlifting at his last school in Chicago. So he was an American, which may have accounted for an extra dollop of drama. He had an easy, confident way about him that had nothing to do with conceit or reckless rebellion. He was also fun and funny. He could squeeze a smile out of a slab of granite. Jim Wheeler had been the class hero before George arrived one late September morning. By noon hour of the following day, nearly every one of the girls had switched allegiance and was planning strategies aimed at snaring George McIsaac.

And of course Jill headed the hungry pack. I may have forgotten to mention that she was beautiful. She had all this flawless olive skin, a pert nose, and a look of wide-eyed innocence and wonder. But most of all I think it was her hair that drew the boys to her. It was long and full, and of that soft and feathery texture that formed a halo when the light was behind her. George was destined, we feared, to be Jill's trophy, and we watched in envy as she cast her fly and prepared to reel him in. They seemed made for each other. Isn't there an almost perfect couple in every high school? It seems to me that there are nearly always two spectacular people who are drawn together, and who find it easy to ignore the fruitless yearnings of the rest of the world.

We girls in Grade 11 kept our furtive longings in check, and laughed a lot, lest anyone think that we were suffering. Jim Wheeler was suffering too—a fact that is obvious to me now, but which, at that particular time, was of no concern at all to any of us. He'd been Jill's major interest until the morning George walked through the door of our classroom, and they'd been a couple for so long—five weeks, maybe—that even I was starting to wonder if she'd given up doing what we then called "playing the field." Everyone envied her beauty and popularity, but most of us also liked her—in spite of the things she did that shocked us. She was cheerful and fun, and seemed to ask nothing in return, except of me, her best friend. From me she asked silence, and she got it. The boys didn't tattle about their escapades with her. Revealing what she did with them would demean them as much as it would her, because one by one they had been discarded. And the uninvolved ones were simply waiting their turn.

Then George arrived. On that first day, Jill told me that those massive shoulders, that powerful chest made Jim Wheeler's lanky good looks seem flimsy, slightly effeminate. And George's almost instant appeal to everyone else fanned her flame. Boys liked him because he was a straightforward, no-nonsense type of person with no apparent hidden agendas. He was also athletic and strong. Rightly or wrongly, boys and men admire those qualities in their friends and heroes. The girls went limp and weak with longing when he smiled at them; and he smiled often—at just about everybody. So, for a short while, most of us felt that we had some sort of a chance with George McIsaac. I thought my own was particularly good. His desk was beside mine in the classroom, so we often exchanged bits and pieces of conversation and a lot of laughs between periods. I was pretty, petite, and I was sure that his eyes were telling me that he liked what he saw.

But not for long. By the end of week two, it was clear that I and all the other girls were to be the losers. He leaned against his locker, arms folded, and talked to Jill in the corridor. They walked round and round the football field at lunchtime, when all the rest of us were eating our cold sandwiches in the bleak cafeteria. When the first snow came, they made angels together in the parking lot.

Jim Wheeler could see how the wind was blowing, and started to pursue Maria Dallas, not wishing to look any more pathetic and discarded than necessary. Maria had had her eye on him ever since Grade 8—

fruitlessly, she had thought—and was happy to oblige, apparently never having heard of the dangers of the rebound.

I watched all this—in the classroom, at dances, in the schoolyard, downtown at the Rialto Café—and my heart was a chunk of clay in my chest. I was seventeen, but never before had I experienced anything like what I was feeling for George McIsaac. I could hardly wait to go to bed at night so that I could start my torrid nighttime daydreams of life with George. I dated him, did simple and innocent things with him—walking on beaches, watching sunsets and moonrises by the seawall, showing my considerable grace and expertise on the dance floor, sharing picnics with him at Hubbards beach. And time after time I lost my virginity to him. I knew how to do every one of those things. Had I not learned all the strategies from someone who'd been there many times before me? I writhed on the bed, wept into my pillow, and lost a lot of sleep.

In the meantime, I waited for Jill to arrive on the scene, *my* scene, with a running commentary on all that was going on. I didn't want to hear any of it, but I also felt a sick compulsion to know everything. I also waited for her to tire of George. Didn't she always eventually grow weary of each of the boys she spent time with? Her motto: use them, drop them, and move on.

But none of those things happened. She stopped phoning me. When we met or when she could spare half an hour from her time with George, she told me nothing. And she didn't tire of George. Weeks, months went by, and things remained the same. There they were: Jill and George, the school's most charismatic and constant couple. I was eaten alive by longing. I was also tortured by the knowledge that George didn't even *know* the person he was so crazy about. He thought she was innocent and perfect. Ha! I knew better. I had lost the love of my life to someone who was unworthy of the prize. I deserved him. She did not. And I was powerless to change things.

Or was I? My daydreams started to unfold into different scenarios. I imagined myself watching

George while one of the boys—Gary Mason, maybe—told him what she'd been doing in her father's car and in some of the old forts of Point Pleasant Park, before he'd arrived. I witnessed George's face as Gary listed the boys who'd screwed her on the mats in the gym equipment room and in the woods by the railway cutting. I imagined the police arriving in the middle of English class and taking her off, preferably in handcuffs, on multiple charges of shoplifting. Always, at the end of the fantasy there was a tender scene in which he looked long into my eyes, and then took me tenderly into his arms, murmuring in his deep gravelly voice, "I should have realized all along that you were the one I really wanted." Then he would brush a lock of hair from my forehead and touch my face with gentle fingers. "You need to respect the person you love," he would say. Then would come his hard hot breath, my sense of his enormous strength, my willing surrender.

I had been privy to Jill's outrageous behaviour for so long that you would have thought I'd be able to do something outrageous myself without fear of the consequences—particularly since what I eventually did seemed so safe, so private, so altogether undetectable. But when the day arrived when I was to do it, the air around me seemed charged with an electrical intensity so strong that even the smallest details of that afternoon have remained with me vividly and in full colour. I'm able to see that in school that day, Mrs. Finkle, our homeroom teacher, had a new perm that made her look fat and forty. I see Maria Dallas and Jim holding hands between their desks, and I notice that her arm is still tanned from last summer and that a silver bangle is showing off the warm brown of her skin. I observe again the initials that someone has carved on my desk—H.R.—no one I know. I smell Jack Hogarty's bubble gum, the floor wax from the weekend's cleaning, the chalk dust that had accumulated since nine o'clock. I notice that Doris Jollimore is wearing socks that don't entirely match. Almost, but not quite. I look at my hands, slender with perfect skin, and see that they are trembling slightly. It is they, after all, that will be doing the deed. When I relive that day, I sense again a rising nausea.

I wrote the letter on a rickety old typewriter that I'd bought second-hand from an ad in the paper. It had been my constant companion since Grade 6. I had to reset the ribbon manually—twisting the reel round and round with my index finger—and a few of the letters were pretty faint. The capital R had the tail broken right off. But it was okay. I taught myself to touch type on it, and this was to be useful for me later on when I searched for summer jobs to help with my tuition at Dalhousie.

When I returned home from school that afternoon, I sat down at my desk and rolled the paper into the machine. It was white, blank, ready. "To whom it may concern:" I started. Then I went on: "Here is information that you might like to have about the girl you are going steady with." I crossed out "might like to have" and substituted the words "should know."

I paused then, my stomach hollow with fear and with guilt. I had kept her secrets safe for so long that it seemed a cataclysmic act to reveal even one of them. But had she not discarded our friendship as casually as she had dropped all those former boyfriends? Yes, she had. Had she done this without explanation of any kind? That is correct. Had I suffered immeasurably as a result? Yes, and I still did. Given her personal history, did she deserve to possess the most attractive boy in Grade 11? No, she most certainly did not. Would it, in fact, be a kindly favour to him to open his eyes to the truth of the matter? I had more difficulty with that one. However, after staring at the wall for maybe forty-five seconds, I answered myself. Yes, it would be doing him a great service.

Then, the preliminaries over with, I started, with considerable relish, to list Jill's past sins. I let myself be free and fulsome in my descriptions of what she had done. I gained this freedom by telling myself that I might not, after all, send that letter. And I could edit it, soften it, later.

I told about her shoplifting episodes. I named stores, described articles she had stolen, some of which she still wore. I recounted lies she had told, listed her deceptions. I told about the frog incident and Gladys Anderson's hysterics. I mentioned other small and secret cruelties. I revealed the methods she used to cheat on exams. Then, saving the frosting until the last, I wrote down the names of all the boys she had slept with—when, where, and small revealing details about the couplings. Feeling purged and empty, barren of all feeling except a niggling itch of fear, I signed it "Anonymous." I reread it, changed nothing, folded it, put it in an envelope, addressed it, stamped it. I took it to the mailbox, running all the way, blanking out my brain as I shoved it through the slot. I think I was afraid that if I slowed down or permitted myself even one conscious thought, I might change my mind. But the letter was gone. The mailbox had swallowed it, and it was irretrievable. I felt a dreary relief. Justice had been done. I also experienced a dull sense of terror that was both suppressed and nameless.

You must be wondering what happened after all of this. By now you may have taken sides. Who are you cheering for? Me? George? Jill? Or maybe one of the bit players: Jim Wheeler, Maria Dallas, poor old Gladys Anderson. Who will win the prize in this unlikely contest? Or is there, after all, a prize to be won?

The day after I sent the letter was like any other. Of course it was. The letter had not yet arrived. Mail can move with the speed of an earthworm in Nova Scotia. Another day passed. Same thing. By then I would have exchanged almost any precious thing I owned for one sleeping pill. I scarcely closed my eyes at night except to intensify the daydreams I allowed myself. George McIsaac and I moving down the aisle after the ceremony, my arms overflowing with calla lilies. Jill in the back pew, eyes averted from the festive panorama. Further scenes of tenderness, warmth, comfort, and savage passion. Jill looking on from afar, in a kind of sidebar, always alone.

On the third day, neither George nor Jill attended school. What could this mean? I had no idea. I was disappointed. I wanted to witness the scorn in George's eyes when—after reading the letter—he would first see Jill enter the classroom. I didn't want their first meeting to take place in some private location where I wouldn't be able to see it.

On the fourth day, it was the same. Disappointment was replaced by fear. I missed two questions in math. I didn't hear Mrs. Finkle when she called my name. I forgot that it was my day to clean the board. My comfortable daydreams gave way to anxious speculation. Maybe they had completed a suicide pact. Maybe he would kill her and then himself. Vividly, in primary colours, I saw the scene: red blood, staring blue eyes, a cobalt sky, and, later, black night. That fourth day was a Friday. I would have to live through forty-eight more long hours until Monday.

On Monday, the weather was perfect—the kind of day that Nova Scotia does best. I could see a small triangle of harbour from my bedroom window, and it was shimmering in the silver light. The day had the kind of clarity that inlanders never see. You could smell approaching spring in the air, even though it was still January.

George and Jill arrived late. We were all in our seats when they slipped in. No, they did not *slip* in. They *entered*. They smiled at Mrs. Finkle, made their apologies, walked down the aisles, heads high, smiling slightly, moving slowly. George sat down in his accustomed seat, across the aisle. He didn't look at me. Jill came down the aisle on my other side, and stopped at my desk. The faint smile died on her face. Standing perfectly still, ignoring the fact that attendance was being taken, she looked me full in the eyes. There was no expression of any kind in her face, and she continued with her empty stare for maybe the eternity of sixty seconds. By that time, I unglued my eyes from hers, and dropped my gaze to the surface of my desk. Then she continued on to the back and her own place.

Neither I nor you will ever know what took place on those two days when George and Jill were absent from school, or during the endless weekend that followed. Only someone with an IQ of 70 could think that Jill wouldn't know who had sent that letter. And my IQ is 140. How could I have thought that the word "Anonymous" would protect me? Apart from the fact that I was the only one who knew everything, my elderly typewriter would have given me away as surely as if I had written the letter in my own hand. But what happened *then,* when they read together the letter written by Anonymous? Did I become the liar and she the lied-upon? Did he rush to protect her from such savage defamation? Or did he believe it all and still love her? None of us had ever seen that kind of love before. Few people ever do. But before a week had passed, I knew that both of them were capable of exactly that.

Neither Jill nor George ever spoke to me again—not once during that long stretch from January to June, nor in the year that followed. In groups, they acted as though I was not there. On school teams or during summer games, no ball was ever thrown to me. On the city bus, if there were two empty seats beside me, they remained standing. They never faced me with what I had done. They simply erased me from their lives. To them, I became a non-person, which is certainly the way I felt. And feeling like a non-person is something that can remain with you forever.

In fact, this is why I'm writing this account of what happened more than fifty years ago. I'm still in conflict and confusion about all of it. She was guilty of all I accused her of. And she had not been loyal to our friendship. Did she not deserve what I did to her? Did I not deserve better than I received? I don't know. Is it necessary for me to focus on an event so old and frayed and troubling, and still experience something that feels like a death? Tell me. Too much time has passed. I need to know.

The Music Festival

Gina DeSilvo looked across the road. Over there, a tall boy was standing on the balcony of his parents' apartment, three floors up from the street. She counted. Same as hers. He was perfectly still. His hands were curled around the railing, and he was staring straight ahead.

Her heart did a little flip-flop. *I can look right into his eyes,* she thought. And yes, she could and did. But he wasn't returning her gaze. The road wasn't wide— just a back lane off North Street. It was easy to see that his eyes were focused on nothing. How could that be? He seemed to be staring directly at her, but there was an absent quality about his eyes that troubled her. Blind? *No. I don't think so.* Something else. She went inside and got a pair of her father's old binoculars. Hiding behind the balcony curtain, she trained them on the boy across the street.

This kid looked as if he had everything going for him. To begin with, his apartment building was classier than hers. Mind you, *classy* wasn't really a word that fitted any of the buildings in this area. Most of the houses were flat faced, flush with the street, and needed a fresh coat of paint. People returning after twenty-five years away in Ontario would look at that street and say, "Ah yes. Halifax." They would say it with a sigh, because in this part of the city—"the City of Trees"—there was no space for even one blade of grass between the front doors and the curbs. No trees *here*.

However, the boy's apartment building was newer than Gina's, and looked less defeated. As for him, he was very tall, with shoulders to match his height. Lots of untidy sandy hair, loose white T-shirt, bare feet. His balcony was the kind you could see through, with long skinny banisters. If he chose to take a sunbath, she could watch.

But this guy wasn't just looking vacant. He was looking miserable. *Vacant with grief,* she thought. She liked to play around with words.

The DeSilvos had moved into their new apartment yesterday. What unbelievable luck to find herself living across the road from that extravagantly cool guy. But maybe he was just visiting—from Toronto maybe, or even California. Yes, probably California. He looked that good.

Gina's father was dead. Or so her mother said. But Gina had her doubts. *Just took off* is what she really thought. Two years ago, he went away. "On a business trip," he said, as he went out the door with his suit-case, forgetting to kiss her goodbye. She was only thirteen then, young enough to kiss; but is anyone ever too *old* for a father to kiss? *Business trip. I just bet.* She'd seen him with lots of women, different ones at different times—at the movies, in restaurants, coming out of bars—and he looked at them with hunger in his eyes. Not the way he looked at Mom. How did he look at her? Irritated. Fed up. Trapped. And this business trip. How can you go on a business trip when you don't have a business? Or any kind of job at all. He was a writer. So-called. A non-writing writer. He had a big old desk in the bedroom for writing his novel. He even had a contract—with a time limit. The publisher had sent him his advance—his Advance Against Royalties, to be exact—but that had been used up a long, long time ago. It hadn't been very big, anyway. The publisher must have guessed that his company wasn't going to see that finished manuscript anytime soon. All Gina ever saw him do at that desk was sharpen pencils and organize paper clips, often sneaking looks at the *Time* magazine that he kept in the top drawer. And gazing at the wall, frowning. Gina's eyes were looking curtained now. She was blinded by her own mind, thinking difficult thoughts.

Her mother, Mrs. DeSilvo, carried them. She worked as a freelance insurance agent, so money wasn't ever a sure thing. One month fantastic. The next month bad. Sometimes it seemed as though everyone already had insurance or didn't want it. So Mrs. DeSilvo didn't exactly carry them. She sort of *dragged* them. But without her, the family would have been at a dead halt. Gina had a younger brother—Mario. Another mouth to feed. And almost entirely useless at washing dishes or making his own lunch. *Mom's fault. She should make him.* He's not paralyzed. He could butter bread. Or stack dishes.

Gina figured her mother should keep an eye on Mario's behaviour—or his *lack* of behaviour. How did she think her husband got to be so self-centred and lazy? His own mother. That's how. She used to come for a short visit from time to time. She treated her son like a golden idol, praising his talent and his every move, bringing him luxurious gifts, smiling bravely when he spoke sharply to her, plying him with cups of tea and truffles. Asking for nothing in return.

But of course all that had stopped when Gina's dad left—with his biggest suitcase—on his mythical business trip. After all, her grandmother had come to visit *him,* not *them.*

Then Gina gazed once more at the balcony opposite her. *I bet that guy across the street helps with the housework. He looks almost too perfect to be true.*

The guy across the street was sixteen, and his name was Tim McGee. He was staring into space, thinking. *Let it hurry up and be tomorrow so that I can remember it—or forget it—instead of worrying about it.* The music festival was in full swing. That afternoon, he'd be playing on that big grand piano with twenty-three others in the seventeen-and-under category. His birthday was last week, so he just missed being in the fifteen-and-under group. This happened every year. Therefore, the piece he had to play was always very difficult—*too* difficult, in fact. He knew that. But neither his teacher nor his parents would ever admit it. Too long, too much to remember. Too many excruciatingly quick sections, with a lot of trills. Big chords, going very fast. Fancy gymnastic finger work. He liked the piece. He felt good as he played it, and for about five minutes after he finished. But he shut his eyes to keep from thinking of the months it had taken him to learn it, to get it *right.* And in that long interval, no hours for basketball practice, no way to get on the team. Not much TV at all. No time for hanging out down at Park Lane or going to movies with his friends.

It wasn't Tim's idea to take piano lessons. It hadn't ever been what he wanted, although he knew that he loved music—to listen to, to dance to, to keep in the background of his head. But in Grade 3, a travelling music consultant had swept into his school and given the kids a lot of tests. He'd sent Tim home with a note.

It said, "Your son has perfect pitch and an unusual sense of rhythm. He is very responsive to melody and harmony. He exhibits unique musical potential. This talent should be developed."

His mother read the note aloud to Tim and his father. Late that night, Tim could hear them talking and talking. The next day, when he came home from school, there was an old second-hand piano in the living room, taking up a lot of space and looking pretty chipped and ugly—but freshly tuned, that very morning. "You'll start lessons on Monday afternoon, next week," said his mother. His father smiled proudly. Tim was their only child. All their eggs were in one basket.

From Grade 3 to Grade 11, Tim took lessons twice

a week, and practised an hour a day. Around festival times and before recitals, it was two hours a day. He was certainly good; there was no doubt about *that*. It just didn't happen to be what he'd choose to be doing. But his teacher, Miss Sims—accustomed to students who knew only too well how to mutilate the music of the masters—was ecstatic. "With application, with deeply rooted ambition," she said to Mr. and Mrs. McGee, "he could easily end up on the concert stage. He could *make it* in the music world." She hadn't made it herself. Tim was her one hope for vicarious glory. "Don't ever let him stop," she added.

"Don't worry," said his father. "That will never happen."

Every once in a long while Tim would summon up enough courage to say something like "I'd kind of prefer to do soccer this year instead of music lessons,"

or

"Basketball practice is four days a week, including Mondays. I really think I could make the basketball team if I dropped music,"

or

"I wish I had some free time to just unwind. I feel kind of pushed."

The responses would come thick and fast, his parents interrupting each other in order to be sure that all their views were expressed.

"It's too big a talent to neglect."

Who says? Says who?

"Miss Sims says you can make it to the top."

What's the top? What's good about it? Wherever it is, I don't want to go there.

"We spent all that money on the piano and the lessons."

Then sell the piano. Stop the lessons.

"We're so proud of you. Don't disappoint us."

This last one has been the hardest one to cope with. It has always been the one to shut him up. He'd return to his scales, his finger exercises, his arpeggios, his chords. He'd feel tired enough to die.

Tim hadn't made these feeble suggestions very often. If you're trapped in a metal cage with a big steel padlock on the door, you know you can't get out. And after a while, you stop rattling the door.

But as he stood now on the balcony staring off into nothing—looking right into the eyes of Gina DeSilvo without knowing it—he was planning his whole future. *Tonight he was going to attack the usual arguments head-on.* He only had one more year of high school. It was his last chance to get on the basketball team, to try some soccer, to goof around with the kids on Friday afternoons, to find himself a girlfriend and go to the movies with her or maybe just walk in Point Pleasant Park and *talk*. Or whatever. He figured it was his last chance to be young.

So he was talented. He knew this to be true. He'd heard other kids attack the piano as though they were chopping wood, all the notes perfect, but with no feeling, no sense of what music really was. Too loud and too fast. What Tim thought of as "kill-the-keys playing." If he didn't make it as a concert pianist, he'd end up teaching those awful kids. He'd sooner be a garbage collector. And being a concert pianist wouldn't be much better. Dear God, practising five hours a day, crazed with nerves before every concert. In fact, nervous as a cat before every *lesson*—

with those high-powered teachers they were threatening him with. He'd overheard his parents discussing the possibility of the Royal Conservatory of Music in Toronto. He thought about the obligation he'd feel toward his parents as they squeezed out the money for those teachers.

No, thank you. It had to stop somewhere, and it had to be *now*—before he got permanently locked into a position he didn't want. It would happen tonight when the festival was over. Whether he won or lost.

Tim had not yet won a trophy in the festival. Each year, the tension in his music teacher and his parents mounted to something close to hysteria. Their desire for him to win took precedence over schoolwork, family times (*what* family times?), meals, sports, friends, rest. Each year, with limitless hours of work, he learned to play the required piece perfectly and with an unusual depth of feeling. Then, four days before the festival started, his nerves would click in, would take over. His knees would wobble. His hands would shake. His mouth would be dry. At the performance, his fingers would turn numb and uncoordinated, runs would be sloppy, wrong notes would appear out of nowhere. The adjudicators knew he was good. But they could never give him first place.

He always had to spend the next week comforting his teacher, comforting his parents. No one seemed to consider his own need to be comforted.

But at last he'd had enough. *Enough*. This afternoon would be his final performance. He knew, in some oblique and penetrating way, that this time he'd really make it a reality. He'd follow through. Tomorrow, as the saying goes, would be the first day of the rest of his life. He smiled at this hackneyed thought.

He felt as weightless as a dandelion seed, blowing in the wind. During that exact same minute, he felt as sturdy as a concrete wall.

The misery went out of Tim's face, and something else took its place. It was strong and it was visible. His eyes returned to reality and found themselves staring into the snapping black eyes of Gina DeSilvo. Shyly, tentatively, they each raised a hand in greeting. At that moment, although they didn't know it, both of them said the same thing. Tim said it out loud, very firmly. Gina whispered it. What they said was, "Everything's going to be all right."

My Heroine, Murphy Brown

December 22

To my future readers:

Since this is the very first day for writing this account of my life, I feel I should introduce myself.

My name is Yvette Adonis, and I am fourteen years old. Fourteen is an age that my mother would tell you is neither fish nor fowl. When my father is in a jocular mood, which isn't very often, I've heard him say that I'm between the devil and the deep blue sea. The reason he isn't jocular very often is that he has "a very demanding job," which is the way my mother describes it. I've also heard her mutter to herself (but maybe hoping someone will hear) that she has a demanding job, too, what with having three other kids younger than me, and no one crowding around to help her with the dishes or the laundry or even to pick their junk up off the floor. She's usually in a good mood, but she does a lot of muttering. My father isn't what you'd call crabby, but he also isn't what you'd call a ray of light around the house—or even very *useful.* A lot of the time he just stares off into space, with worry lines between his eyebrows. He owns a real estate business, and my mom has told me that houses aren't moving. That's the way she puts it. I know exactly what she means, but it seems to me that it's the people who aren't moving, not the houses.

You will notice that I have a very odd name, Yvette Adonis. I really wonder what my parents had in mind. Adonis was the Greek god of love. Dad's parents came over from Greece to live in Canada a long time ago, bringing their name with them. Yvette, as any dummy can tell you, is a French name. I'm not suggesting for one second that I should have been named Venus Adonis (ha ha ha), but why tack the French onto the

Greek, when we don't have one single drop of French blood in our veins? The name is bound to confuse people. I asked my mother why they called me that, but she just shrugged (one of her many annoying nervous tics) and said she liked the name.

You will notice that I'm very articulate. I'm using that word because I hear it so often. People are forever saying, "Just listen to that Yvette Adonis. She's so articulate." The reason I'm so articulate is that I had to start being old at a very early age. Being the oldest of four kids is quite a burden. They're *way* younger than I am—two, four, and six years old, to be precise. It didn't take me long to realize that four kids were too many for my mother's capabilities. Therefore I undertook to do the really demanding work of reading them stories and teaching them to talk so that Mom would have time for the more straightforward chores of dishwashing and meals and laundry. You've noted, I'm sure, that everything I've done with those kids has involved language. Any meathead could get to be articulate who spent as much time talking and reading as I have.

This isn't a real diary. No, indeed. It's really my autobiography, and I'm writing on lined pads from the dollar store. The pages have holes along the side so I can put them in a binder when I get enough of them filled up. And I've already used up three and a half pages (every second line, in order to give my editors lots of room for comment and the odd correction). I hope to have all my binders published as a book when I turn twenty-one—i.e., when I become an adult. That will give the Canadian public a clear picture of what it's like to be a child and a teenager. But at the rate I'm going, the combined entries will fill up about six hundred book pages. So I'd better stop right this minute.

I said I was fourteen. Actually I'm nearly fifteen. I'll be fifteen in February. Now you know who I am. Tomorrow we can get down to business.

December 31

I started this first notebook during the holidays so I'd have lots of time to write in it. What a joke. My best friend, Helena, keeps bugging me to try out our skis on the Gorsebrook Hill, or go out to the Halifax Shopping Centre to spend her Christmas money, or to come over to her house to watch TV. I agree to do all those things because there's too much bugging going on around here, and the best thing to do is to get out. Mom bugs me to keep the kids out of her hair if she's trying to centre her mind on one of her crazy gourmet recipes, or when she's working on Dad's financial books, or when she tries to sneak fifteen minutes for a shower. I guess she figures if I have a holiday, she should be able to cash in on it. Dad bugs me to turn down the sound on the TV or my radio if he's in the middle of his staring-out-the-window routine. I can't see why it needs to be quiet if all he's doing is looking at the Fergusons' front veranda, but Mom says he's thinking. I'd say he's worrying about houses moving, but maybe he finds that more pleasant if it's quiet.

Of course if houses aren't moving, there's not much money coming in, and this is a big family. You'll notice that although Helena got money for

Christmas, I didn't. I don't know why Mom and Dad kept having kid after kid after kid once they got started again. Eight years is a long gap between me and the others. I was almost an only child. What an opportunity lost. You'd think someone could have explained to them about birth control. It wasn't exactly a new invention at the time—or *times*—when they needed it.

Tonight is New Year's Eve. Mom and Dad are going to a party at the Dickinsons'. I'm supposed to make sure that the kids don't hassle the babysitter to death. I don't see why she can't do that herself, at $5 per hour. Nobody's offering *me* any money. I'm not allowed to babysit till I'm fifteen. Mom says it's too big a responsibility. In about one and a half months, the tide will turn. Then I'll become both rich and free.

I'm writing this in the afternoon, before I'm required to do slave labour in the evening. If I get a free half hour tonight, I'm going to write up my New Year's Resolutions.

Later:

The kids have gone to bed. So have I. Or sort of.
Here are my New Year's Resolutions:

1. To try not to be so crabby with Mom.
2. To clean up my desk so there'll be room for me to
   write on it again.
3. To become beautiful before I hit sixteen. At the
   moment I have four pimples, and when those go,
   probably four more will erupt. My hair is sort of
   greasy, although it's naturally curly, which I recognize as a plus. I'm getting pretty good breasts, but
   I'm also getting a fat middle. So I'm looking less
   like a Barbie doll and more like a large cylinder.
4. To try to be more like TV's Murphy Brown,
   who is beautiful, witty, self-assertive, and full of
   marketable brains. I watch shows on the rerun
   channel, like *Dick Van Dyke, The Mary Tyler
   Moore Show,* and of course all the Bill Cosby
   ones. Even though the shows are very, very old,
   Murphy Brown is very, very cool. I've chosen
   her as my role model. As well as a career

woman, she's also a mother, but I'm not sure I'll go that route. I feel like I've been a mother too long already. Of course she's a blond, but later on I can bleach my hair. Helena says Murphy's too old to be a role model, but I don't have to listen to what she says. See? Already I'm being self-assertive. Murphy Brown is really Candice Bergen, who may actually be slow-moving and gentle—and of course by now as old as the Pyramids—but I don't think of her that way. To me she's Murphy—tough, gorgeous, a professional woman, feisty.

Happy New Year to all my future readers.

Yvette

January 1

It's 8 p.m. and already I've blown Resolution #1. I did get to start work on #2, but before I'd even cleared the *top* layer of junk off the mountain of garbage on my desk, my mother appeared and made a statement that so completely blew my mind that both #1 and

#2 were bombed to extinction. Listen to this. Here is what happened:

"Yvette," she said. I'll try to dig her exact words out of my memory. "Today we're in a brand-new year. It can be a time of fresh starts for everyone. Therefore I want to share with you a new beginning in my own life."

My heart sank like a stone. Another baby, I thought. But no. Still—it was almost as bad.

"I'm forty years old," she said, "and I feel that it's time I began to establish some kind of career for myself. I want something more fulfilling than keeping your father's books. I've been making secret plans about this for a long time, but I'm ready now to go public with it."

A career! Seems to me she's starting a career when she's right on the brink of getting the old-age pension.

I almost screamed at her. In fact, maybe I did. "What?" I yelled. "What *career*" (I could feel myself sneering) "are you planning to have?" I asked myself what she was fit for: work in a laundry, backstage in a restaurant, up front in a daycare centre, in some windowless room adding up columns of figures. Just like at home, in fact.

"I'm going to be working at the local TV station," she said. Then she waited for my reaction.

She got it. I'm not 100 percent proud of my response.

"Doing *what?*" I yelled again. "Vacuuming the studio?"

She held her head up so high that her neck seemed to be coming right out of her sweater. "I'll be reading the five o'clock news," she said.

"You'll be *what?*" I shouted. "*On TV?* Right there where all my friends can see you? Mom! You're an old woman! Don't do this to me! Turn it down!"

"I start tomorrow," she said.

I sat down. The shock was very intense. Not only was my mother about to make a public fool of herself. I also (very swiftly) worked out who'd be feeding those kids at five-thirty while she was down at the studio humiliating the entire family.

She could read my mind. "I'll be making money, you know," she said. "I've arranged for a woman to come in between three and six to feed the kids and look after them. The rest of us can eat when I get home—at about six-thirty."

"Three to six? You said you'd read the news at five. What's with all this three-hour stuff?"

"I won't just read it," said my new mother. "I'll also have to prepare the material and do post mortems afterwards. We need the money. And I want something more interesting than cleaning and cooking and diapers." (Sammy, who is two, looks like he's going to postpone toilet training until high school.)

I have to do my homework. I'll talk more about this disaster tomorrow. I long to be Murphy Brown, who could dispose of this problem with a flick of her wrist.

January 2

At five o'clock we all huddled around the TV set to watch the news. All except me. I stood against the opposite wall and wished for oblivion. I felt as though I was about to witness my own death. My whole hand was over my face except where I could look out between the fingers. I didn't want to see more than was absolutely necessary.

She was good. I could tell she was a little bit nervous, but I don't think anyone else would know. She had on her navy blue suit and her high-necked white blouse—somewhat nun-like, but nothing to shame me beyond recovery. But someone had better teach her how to pep up her wardrobe, and the obvious choice for that job is me. She stumbled a bit on Herzegovina, and paused a split second too long before mentioning the name of the emperor of Japan, but my totally unrecognizable mother was great. She didn't look old. Maybe you look less old behind an anchor desk than in front of a hot stove, or perhaps they did the fountain-of-youth thing with a ton of makeup. Her hair is blond and sort of straight with a bend on the end of it. I was proud. I felt a lump in my throat. Dad looked wide awake for the first time in about four months. The kids were all cheering, except for Sammy, who kept patting the screen with his sticky hands and yelling, "Mama! Mama!"

January 3

Just a quick report. In school today I discovered that I had achieved instant fame. I even forgot my pimples for a while and the fact that I'm built like a cylinder. I tried as hard as I could to look bored when girls kept coming up to me and saying, "Why can't *my* mother do something special?" or "What's it like living with a celebrity?" I'd just sigh a little, and say, "It's not always easy."

January 8

I've skipped a few days. I've been too busy to be writing the story of my life. I just looked at the final sentence of my last entry. "It's not always easy." *Prophetic words.* That woman who comes here from three to six is nice. In fact, she's *very* nice. But you'll notice that she leaves at six. At about six twenty-five, in sweeps Mom, panting from her three hours with the media, and we're all hungry. She has her arms full of groceries, and she plunks them down on the kitchen counter and sighs a lot. The kids have been missing her, so she does all her meal preparations with Sammy clinging to her left leg and Julian yelling his day's news at her—the latest report from Grade 1. I give Jackson (the four-year-old) his bath, and let him splash around in the bubbles while I go to collect Sammy. I don't have time to read them stories any more. Dad makes the very big mistake of asking, "When's dinner?" and Mom snaps back at him, "I can't do everything at once! If you're hungry, go eat one of the kids' arrowroot cookies!" She scoops up Julian and gives him a big hug, but I can see that she's got two deep lines between her eyebrows—just like Dad's. She doesn't look young any more.

That's what it's like around here. Dad has gone back to staring out the window. I've started a diet for the forty-fifth time. Mom looks like she's running a marathon race and can see that she's not winning. The boys are okay, but why couldn't any of them have been girls, and maybe *older*, so that they wouldn't be so totally useless? More and more I'm wishing I was Murphy Brown with her glamorous life and her snappy comebacks and her ability to charge through life like a bulldozer. I haven't cleared off my desk yet.

January 12

Not only is there no time to read. There's also no time to write.

January 22

Today Mom came home at her usual time, but she had a couple of medium pizzas with her instead of bags of groceries. She smiled at all of us as though she meant it. She hugged every member of the family and looked very cheerful. She also had a determined expression on her face that looked familiar to me, but I couldn't quite place it. She opened up the pizza box and divided it among the three plates that I'd put on the table. After we'd all finished our meal, she stood up—as though she planned to make a speech. Which is exactly what she did.

"I'm announcing a new regimen," she said. *"I can't do all of this alone.* Julian, I'm going to teach you how to fold laundry tomorrow. That'll be your own very special job. Jackson, you'll be in charge of picking up all the toys before bedtime. I know you'll be so good at that. Gordon" (she shot my father a piercing and oddly recognizable look) "I thought we could spend a few hours together this weekend while I teach you how to make three simple casseroles. And I'd like you to take over the grocery shopping, at least until those houses start moving. I'll supply you with lists. Yvette, you're pretty useful already, but maybe you could come shopping with me on Saturday for some clothes with a little more flair." Then she added, "I'd like to thank all of you in advance for your co-operation."

She stood up there like a sergeant major, and I had to suppress a desire to salute—or maybe to clap. After all, I was the only one who got brownie points. Julian looked very proud and pleased to have a special job, and Jackson started cruising around the living room, picking up toys. As I walked up the stairs with Sammy for his bath and bedtime story, I could see Mom and Dad seated at the kitchen table with recipe books spread out in front of them. Dad was looking pretty confused and serious, but I also knew there was no way he could buck the plans of that strong-willed woman.

Mom kept reminding me of someone. Who was it? It was really bothering me that I didn't know. I'd read all three stories to the boys and tucked them into bed before I realized who it was. You guessed it. It was *Murphy Brown*. Mom even *looks* a lot like her. She's a sort of softer, gentler version of her, but she has that same determination and readiness to walk on her own path. And let's face it, the same ability to manipulate the people who can help her to do that.

February 15

Well, you can see that a whole lot of time has swept by since I last wrote parts of this autobiography. But the fact is that I think I'm going to stop writing my life story. I always thought I was going to be a famous writer because everyone said I was so articulate. But what I always really wanted to be was a musician. I'm fifteen now, and I'm babysitting a lot of *other* people's kids. That means I'm earning tons of money. I'm saving all of it till I have enough to buy Brian O'Hara's old guitar. He's in Grade 11, and he has a new one. Then I'll learn to play it. He said he'd teach me. He doesn't seem to mind that I'm still built like a cylinder. But if my mom can turn from a household drudge into a four-star anchorwoman in a month and a half, I bet I can turn into a musician in no time at all.

I've been pretty good at #1 of my New Year's Resolutions. I'm not as crabby with Mom as I used to be. My desk is still piled high with junk, so #2 is a write-off. I'm no closer to being beautiful, so there goes #3. I'm certainly not one bit like Murphy Brown, so maybe that obliterates #4. But on the other hand, I live with Murphy Brown's clone now, so maybe some of her smarts will rub off on me. And my genes will be on my side, even though I do have black curly hair.

Things are really looking up around here. I even heard on TV yesterday—on the five o'clock news, to be exact—that houses are starting to move again in this area. And even if they don't move very fast, I've noticed that my dad has bought about six new cookbooks, a cool new red electric egg beater, and a gadget for pressing garlic. And he doesn't stare out the window nearly as much any more.

Escape Route

Allow me to introduce myself. My name is Winthrup McDermid Winslow. Winthrup Winslow. Can you imagine a woman calling her new baby such a name? But no. It would have been my dad who did the naming. And my brother's name is just as absurd. He's called Anderson Fairchild Winslow. That's not because he was a fair child. Those crazy names are last names of our illustrious ancestors. Who seem to have been doing brilliant things ever since the time of the flood.

Which brings me around to the subject of my father. The thing I've kept asking myself, even when I was just a little kid, is "How did he get that way?"

Now I'm fifteen and I ask it more often—nearly every day. How can a person be charming and clever and widely respected, and also cruel and thoughtless and ungrateful—every single one of those things. How can he listen so attentively—and with such softness in his face—(I've *seen* it)—to other people, and yet almost never listen, *really* listen to his own family. When we're talking to him, he gets up and walks around, sometimes right out of the room, drumming his fingers on the back of something he's carrying, or he picks up a newspaper or the TV guide and scans it while we're speaking. It's as if he feels that what we have to say isn't worth his full attention. If you ever have the courage to say, "Hey, Dad, listen to me, will you?" he says, "I'm listening, I'm *listening,* for God's sake," as he flips over the pages of *The Financial Post.*

Every once in a while, a *long* while, he does actually sit down and have a conversation with me. He looks me in the eye and even asks questions about what I'm talking about. Once I remember that he said, "Tell me more about that." I don't think that the topic was in any way serious or important. I don't remember that part. That day I had a whole lot of trouble with what I was saying. I was fourteen, which is pretty old, but I got all tightened up in my throat and was scared like crazy that I was going to cry, right in the middle of that history-making conversation. I had to keep watching the light shining on his bald head, or the way the little hairs showed in his nostrils, or the fidgeting he was doing with a loose thread on the sleeve of his sweater. That way I could answer his next question without bursting out sobbing. All that *attention* was breaking me right up, even though part of me noticed that he was doing most of the talking—advice, reminiscences, admonitions. But it's one of the happiest memories I have. I was so busy trying to keep from bawling like a damn baby that I missed half of what he was saying. The next day he got mad when he discovered I'd forgotten some of his monumentally wise words and sage advice. But his anger wasn't successful in wiping out the pleasure of that conversation. You'll notice that I still remember it.

My dad's a CEO—which stands for chief executive officer. He's the big boss of a large successful computer company. That's what every one of us is supposed to be, too. Successful, I mean. All three of us, even my sister, Olivia, who you'd think he might lay off of because she's only a girl. That's one of his very favourite expressions: "… only a girl" or "… just a woman." He doesn't expect Mom to be successful. In fact, he hopes like anything that she'll never do anything that stupid. Stupid, because the smart thing for her to do is be his perfect, marvellous wife, and nothing else, for the whole of her goddamn life.

A perfect, marvellous wife doesn't have a career, or even just a *job*. She stays home and makes sure that the house looks like a furniture store display window, and that there's not a speck of dust, or a pile of magazines unaligned, or a single dirty dish in the sink. She's also supposed to praise him for his hard work and his large paycheque, and to swing elaborate, elegant dinner parties for him and his colleagues and their boring-as-pablum wives. Also, cocktail parties where everyone yells at everyone else, and where the only time anyone really looks at you is when you're passing one of the plates of fancy canapés, which never fill you up but which take my mom about ten years to prepare.

We always used to be hauled in to be *shown* at the parties when we were little. Dad would come up and look at us tenderly and gather all three of us into his arms and say, "I want you to meet the three people who really run this family," and then kiss each of us on the tops of our heads. He only did this when there were people around. The big father act. He stopped doing this as soon as Anderson—Andy—got to be eleven or twelve. Fathers aren't supposed to hug their sons once they get to be that age. Did you know that? Instead, they slap them hard on the back and remind them to be brave and strong and to *achieve* (win all the races on field day, get on the honour roll at school, and later on take the prettiest girl to the school dance). And also be obedient, silent, and— even at age eight or nine—a *man*.

Mom, now, I guess she was the prettiest girl at the school dance. She must be forty-five, but she's still beautiful, if you don't count that little vertical line between her perfectly plucked eyebrows. No fat on *her*. No sloppy old jeans on weekends. Not one hair out of place. Yes, dear. No, dear. Exactly the kind of woman he wants her to be. Even I, a boy of fifteen, know about the Women's Movement. But it would be easy to think that she'd never even heard of it. Probably scared stiff of stepping out of line—just like the rest of us. Her kids, I mean. Us. To whom she is a kind and loving mother.

A lot of the guys' mothers are driving their husbands bonkers by *asserting* themselves and joining women's groups and talking about their rights. Some of them even have big jobs and bring home paycheques as big as their husbands'. If Mom did that, she'd be dead before you could turn around three times. I figure it's harder to push a woman around if she's making more than you are, or if she's someone else's boss in some cushy office in a tall concrete tower. We live in Toronto, where there's a lot of tall concrete towers.

Dad was born in Rosedale. Rosedale is an ancient section of Toronto that is full of old stately homes and stiff-necked, respectable people. No convenience stores in Rosedale. No untidy vacant lots for playing noisy games of softball or kick-the-can. Everybody's *inside*, polishing their manners or their priceless family collections of antique silver.

Rosedale people never forget who they are. They're so convinced that they're the absolute top dogs that it doesn't even scare them to think about the giant mansions in North Toronto, which are so huge that if someone blew a police whistle as hard as he could in the west end of the building, you'd never be able to hear it if your room was at the east end. But even if a Rosedale house is small, it's still *best.* We're not just talking about money here. We're talking about *blood.*

Mom came from the Beaches. The Beaches suddenly became trendy around the time I was a baby, and now the place is full of rich baby boomers and DINKS—which means Double Income No Kids. The Beaches weren't always like that. Mom wasn't exactly wrong-side-of-the-tracks material, but pretty close, pretty damn close. Especially to anyone who happened to live in Rosedale. When Dad married her, I bet she realized she was going to be hauled up by her bootstraps. I figure she knew from the moment she felt that ring slide onto her finger that the only safe thing for her to do was be perfect.

Sometimes I wish I could ask Mom how she feels about being a perfect Rosedale wife—like how life in Rosedale stacks up beside life in the Beaches. But let's face it—you don't go around asking your mother if she enjoys being a doormat. Not when you know how much she loves her children. Not when you know it would be impossible for her to be a different kind of wife. For one thing, she has Grandma to cope with.

Grandma has always lived in Rosedale. Even when she was a kid—if you can imagine anything back that far—she lived on Cluny Drive and went to a girls' private school. Same with Grandpa, except he went to Upper Canada College, which is only for boys. But he was dead before I was born, so he doesn't count. Or maybe he counts more than anything or anyone else, in a roundabout way. But Grandma went to Bishop Strachan School, and therefore always had those inflexible Anglicans propping her up, as well as all the laws of solemn excellence in Rosedale. That's a pretty formidable combination.

Every Sunday, the five of us—me, Andy, Olivia, and my parents—get all decked out in our best clothes and go to church, even though Andy's twenty and sometimes makes the mistake of thinking he has some control over his life. After that, we have noonday dinner at Grandma's. We've been doing this for so long that if one of us suddenly decided to stay home, the stars would fall right out of the sky.

Dinner at Grandma's is dignified and quiet, just the way we're supposed to be in our own house. The table is icy shiny, satin smooth, with dinky little placemats, and the silver is never tarnished or the glasses smudgy. A maid in some kind of soundless shoes appears out of the swinging door and removes the empty dishes and brings new ones. In her black uniform with its white eyelet apron and collar, she's like something out of an old TV rerun, and her face is as expressionless as a statue's. Once I winked at her when no one was looking, and her sweet pale face turned a fiery red. Not pink. Red. She's a scholarship student at U. of T., from Nova Scotia. She's so pretty that I can't even keep my mind on my food, and I'm someone who's always hungry. Her name is Sarah. Sarah calls each of us boys Master Winslow, and calls Olivia Miss Olivia. But we all call her Sarah.

Sarah wears her uniform when she serves us, but when she goes to her classes she wears a skirt and navy blue blazer. Grandma won't let her be seen leaving the house in jeans. The family guard dog has more freedom than Sarah has—and certainly a more respected pedigree.

Grandma is tall and slender, with a very large bosom. When you embrace her (not hug—Grandma is not a hug kind of person) you crash into that huge firm chest before you touch any other part of her. I hate that. Never mind. We only have to do it at Christmas and on her birthday. Embracing isn't required at Sunday dinner. Twice a year I can handle. She stands so straight that you'd think her neck must have a steel rod up the middle. She wears turtleneck blouses and two-piece wool suits, or one of her many high-necked black dresses with a lot of pearls resting on that massive bosom. The high collars must be to hide her wrinkled old neck. I've seen it when she comes to breakfast in her cashmere dressing gown. There, at the head of the polished table, is that neck, visible to all those who choose to look at it.

Not that we go to breakfast all that often, but I stayed with her once when Andy had chickenpox, for two whole weeks. By the time I got home, even my father looked good to me for a couple of days. That woman is so full of instructions and opinions and disapproval that the whole time I was there I felt like some sort of undesirable animal—a mangy stray, certainly not a pet. I once overheard someone say that she pushed Grandpa around like a pawn on a chess-board, and that by the time he was fifty he had no more energy left to cope with all that shoving, so he just up and died of a heart attack. Tired of trying to measure up. I can imagine the same thing happening to me at thirty, if something cataclysmic doesn't happen soon to break the terrible Rosedale pattern that has such a stranglehold on my father. Funny— neither Andy or I seem to be willing to fit into the mould. Andy says he wants to *get out* the minute he can do it, but right now he's in pre-law before going to Osgoode Hall, and has to stay put until he earns enough money to support himself.

Me, now, I want something even worse. Not just to get out and stay out, but to do something entirely different from all those Rosedale forebears. I even feel kind of uneasy about saying it out loud when I'm alone, or even now on paper. But I'm going to say it anyway. I want like crazy to be a garage mechanic. What I feel for engines and motors and the whole beautiful construction of a car is what many people seem to feel about a variety of other things. What a surgeon feels about the vast, convoluted collection of muscles and blood vessels just before he makes his first cut. What a lawyer feels when he walks into court with a file full of intricately documented arguments under his arm. What the photographer feels when a $3,000 camera is placed in his hands. What an artist feels when confronted by a spectacular view or the bone structure of a lovely woman. Awe and respect and also a very intense focus is what I'm talking about.

You can probably see at a glance what my chances are of becoming a first-class garage mechanic—

spending my days tracing the sources of a car's ailments, getting my hands and my overalls black with grease, using my skills to get that engine purring again and ready to fly. Those chances are about as slim as if I announced to my father that I wanted to become a male prostitute. Don't worry—I've thought about ways I might make it happen. For instance, I could join the army and learn my skills at the expense of the Canadian government. But no. My father, providing he could accept the military route instead of the legal or medical or political route, would somehow manoeuvre me into a commission (don't ask me how, but I know he could do it), and I'd end up as a major before I even knew what was happening. And majors don't spend their careers staring at the underbellies of cars.

Or I could run away. But this would break my mother's heart, and would create such a degree of rage in my father and grandmother that the reverberations would reach as far as I chose to run, and would last as long as my whole life. I'm not up to that. My stomach churns into a ball of ice just thinking about it.

No. My father—ignoring my track record of middle-of-the-road exam results—will somehow *impel* me into some university or other, where I will be forced to learn things that are of little interest to me, backed up by an intellect that is good enough for what I want out of life, but not nearly sharp enough for any of the careers that my father has in mind for his younger son. Like law, of course, forgetting that my memorizing skills are so feeble that I couldn't even get parts in school plays. Or medicine, ignoring all those nerves and organs and bones I'd have to learn about. If I was a doctor, the sole thing I'd be good at would be the bedside manner. My only super-good marks are in English and French. And what in God's name, my father has often pointed out, can a successful man do with either of those?

It is necessary for my father to be proud of his children. If he didn't already know this, his mother would tell him so. Can you picture him meeting a couple of his friends or colleagues for a game of golf, and saying to them, "Yesterday Winthrup fixed the fuel line on a '98 Sentra and adjusted the brakes. And during his lunch break he wrote a poem."

Not on your life. It's an impossible scenario. He wants to be able to say, "Yesterday Winthrup performed a triple bypass on the governor general." Or "Last week Winthrup won his court case. Which one? Oh, you know. The one involving a multiple rape and murder. Got him off. No one thought it could be done. But that son of mine can do anything. Chip off the old block." Then he'd make birdie, with the flawless form for which he is so renowned.

Last month at Grandma's, I noticed Andy scrutinizing Sarah while she was serving dessert. Scrutinizing with a recognizable degree of tenderness. Oho! I thought, and an unidentified stab of hope attacked my midsection. Why? I asked myself the same question. And the answer came back: I have no idea. Andy got up from the table and opened the middle window behind the tea wagon. "Spring," he said. A flow of mild air touched our faces.

So I've been watching Sarah and Andy a lot lately. They steal looks at each other whenever we're over at

Grandma's. What else do they steal, I wonder? She lives in a tiny room on the third floor. Even though Andy is twenty, he'd never dare walk over those squeaky floors and up that creaky staircase to see her. Or whatever. You don't stop being scared of your father and grandmother just because you're twenty.

But something is going on. I know it. The colour of Sarah's cheeks comes and goes, ranging from rosy to pale and back to pink again, depending on who she's serving and whether she can see Andy. More and more she's having difficulty keeping her face in the blank mask she's trained herself to wear. Last Sunday, I looked across the table and could see that Olivia was watching, too. Over six feet of mahogany, she and I smiled at each other.

Yesterday I skipped school for the first time in my life. Once I was out of sight of the house I hot-footed it to the university, arriving early enough to take a careful look around. Where to go if I wanted to spy on those two? Where, indeed? That morning, they'd both set out at separate times, probably with their lunches stuffed into their backpacks. I'd seen Sarah pass the corner fifteen minutes before Andy left. Where would they have their picnic? I looked around at the acres of green grass, the places good for sitting. The steps of Vic? The quad at University College? By the war memorial behind Hart House? Under the trees near St. Michael's? This wasn't going to be easy.

I walked round and round the likely areas. It was April, and unusually warm. I decided to ignore the shady areas. Hole or no hole in the ozone layer, sunscreen or no sunscreen, Canadians were tired of ice and snow and would opt for sunny places. I had noted that Sarah was wearing a red kerchief around her neck. I scanned the campus, hoping that my eye might pick up a spot of red.

There she was, over near the war memorial—sitting cross-legged on her navy blazer, a pile of books on the grass, her paper bag open, her face raised to the sun. But alone! I was surprised by my physical sense of deep disappointment. My chest felt caved in and empty. As I sat there hunkered down on the grass among a hundred students, I pondered the foolishness of my expectations. What did I think Sarah—and Andy—could do to create the miracles I longed for? Some kind of love—or even guilty friendship—between those two could surely serve only to solidify the attitudes and goals of my father. Besides, she was due to return to Nova Scotia in August, her master's degree tucked under her arm, headed for those cliffs and tides and beaches that I've read about. Her work was in political science, and she'd even lined up a job for herself in September.

A familiar voice said, "Who are you staring at?" I turned quickly and saw Andy standing behind me, his face grim.

This was not a situation I'd anticipated. I couldn't think of a thing to say. With those five years between him and me, Andy could be as scary as Dad when he was riled up. Like now.

"Dunno," I mumbled.

"C'mon," he growled. "Do better than that."

His anger dragged the truth out of me—the same way Dad's rage could sometimes unravel my secrets.

"I hoped you'd be there," I said, seeing how foolish my dream was. "With her." That's all I could think of to say.

The anger went out of his eyes. He was clearly puzzled. "But why?" he asked.

"I don't know," I said truthfully, as confused as he was.

"Well, *think*," said Andy. "Maybe it'll come to you."

I took a deep breath. What I was going to say sounded 100 percent stupid to me, even before it left my head and got into my voice. "I thought you and she might be an item. I wanted that like anything."

"But why?" said Andy. "I don't understand."

"It was like a door opening," I said, knowing how dopey the words must have sounded to him. People were throwing a Frisbee out there on the field, and all around us was the murmur of voices, and laughter. I thought about how free everyone looked. Maybe they were crazed with fear over essays or exams or their own lives, but it sure didn't look like that to me. The background of all this was so freshly green, and the sky so blue, so clear.

Andy sat down on the grass beside me. "Like how?" he said, not angry at all any more.

I shrugged. "Who knows?" I said. "I didn't work it all out. It's just that lately, when I've seen you looking at each other, I've felt a stupid kind of hope." I stopped talking for a second or two. "But I didn't think about it carefully enough to understand where it all came from."

"What came from?"

"The hope."

"Well, where *did* it come from? And how would it help you? What's the big thing you're looking for?"

"I'm looking for a way to get out from under."

"From under what?"

"*You* know *what!* You're so hungry to get away that I can almost hear you salivating. But that's just getting away. At least you're doing what you want to do. Law and all. But for me, I'm talking about my whole goddamn life."

He was silent for a few moments. He knew about my passion for cars, my impatience with the whole Rosedale scene, the fear and frustration I felt about Dad. He had respect for my desire to work with engines and motors and brakes and mufflers and transmissions. And he'd always agreed that I'd never be permitted to go that route.

"And how did you figure Sarah and I could change all that?" He looked at me carefully.

"I couldn't solve that puzzle before," I said, "but now I think I know what my *unconscious* mind was thinking."

"Which was?"

"If Andy and Sarah are in love, Andy is going to want to follow her when she returns to Nova Scotia. She'll never stay up here in the dirty city if she can go back to that place she's so in love with. I overheard her talking to Mom about the blue sea and the boats and the cool bright air. Besides, she has a job."

"And how, pray tell, could I leave and follow her?"

"You'd just go. You'd love her so much that it would be stronger than your fear of Dad. You'd switch to Dalhousie Law School and just ... *go*."

"And you?"

I smiled. I could feel the sun warm on my face and hands, and I wanted to jump up and dance like a wild person around the lawns and playing fields, skipping and leaping to my own inaudible music. "You're my brother. It'd only be natural to go visit you. And if I put that many miles between me and the people and things I'm afraid of, they mightn't seem so scary any more. And it wouldn't be like running away. It wouldn't break Mom's heart."

"And how would coming down for a visit solve anything?"

"I'd *stay,* dummy. I'd find a way. Not right away. Not this minute. I'd finish school first. I'll get that stupid piece of paper, just in case I'll need it down the road. But then, in Nova Scotia, I'd work up from the bottom pumping gas, go to trade school, get in debt, live to tell the tale." I felt as if I was lighter than helium. I had to grab the grass just to keep from flying right off it.

He turned to me, gave me a long look, and put his big hand on my shoulder. "It could happen," he said, and got to his feet. "I'm late," he added, as he ran off across the lawn to where Sarah was sitting. When she saw him coming, she smiled and waved. Then she raised her head as he came closer, and he bent to kiss her. As I watched, he sat down beside her on the grass, very close. They were pressed together—arm to arm, leg to leg—as they ate their sandwiches out of their brown paper bags, faces turned toward the sun.

Fear

This is what the shrink said. Well, he's not exactly a shrink. He's a *counsellor*. He *counsels*. He advises. He suggests. He asks questions—questions we don't have to answer. He takes us down paths that lead somewhere. His name is Adrien O'Malley. We don't call him Adrien. We call him Mr. O'Malley. "A little distance can be good," he said last week at the end of our first meeting, and then added, "Call me Mr. O'Malley." This isn't what I meant by "what the shrink said." I'll get to that in a minute. I need to tell you some other stuff first.

I'm in this school group that meets every Thursday afternoon. It's the only day when there isn't something like hockey or soccer or art or music, which, of course, I'd be too scared to try out for anyway. It's a free afternoon for all the Grade 8s except us. One day when I was standing outside the staff room, waiting for Mrs. Hugo to hand me out a note, I could hear the teachers talking about our group. I knew it was us they were talking about, because they named names. They called us the VCDs or sometimes VCs. The real VC stands for Victoria Cross, which is a very high level award for bravery (I think maybe you have to die to get it, but I'm not sure. If so, I wouldn't call that much of an inducement if you wanted to collect a chestful of medals). After lurking around outside the staff room and keeping my ears wide open for several days, I was able to discover that VCD stands for Visible and Chronic Defects.

So I'm in this group of kids with visible and chronic defects. Of *course* we're visible. Otherwise, how would they know to put us in the group? And of *course* we're chronic (which basically means on and on and on, forever) or else they could just wait until we stopped being what we are. Our defects are pretty straightforward and easy to define—but apparently not easy to correct. Most of the defects are anger, fear, anxiety, violence. I've been in this school long enough to know that some of the school's scariest bullies have all four of these defects. So you can see right off why it's often so hard to cure a bully of being a bully.

Our group is made up of five boys. This isn't because girls don't have any defects. They have their own VCD group. That's because the school principal thinks we'll feel freer to talk about our problems among our own *gender*. He doesn't like to use the word *sex,* which makes me wonder if he has a chunk of chronic anxiety himself.

My own defect is fear. I've got fear in a big way. I'm so fearful of so many things that even anxiety looks easy. Anxiety is being worried. Being worried all the time is probably not great, but to me it looks easy. Put anxiety and fear on the table together, and figure out the difference between them. Anxiety is walking around on little sharp pebbles in a pair of shoes with very thin soles. Fear is walking on a pile of nails in your bare feet. Terror is when the sharp parts of the nails are sticking straight up. Sometimes I feel terror. Then I don't walk anywhere, in case there might be some nails around.

Apart from walking on nails, I'll give you a short version of what fear is like. It's having a heart that does a lot of hyperactive pounding. It's having a mouth go so dry when someone speaks to you (like a teacher or an uncle or a total stranger asking for directions to the Halifax Shopping Centre) that you don't get a single word out. Or you stutter and tremble, which is worse. It's not ever daring to go to a party or try out for a play or say hello to Annika Setko. It's feeling jittery the minute you wake up in the morning, *before anything even happens.*

The only thing I can do without fear is write. That's because there's just me and the page. I've written in so many journals that I have to keep my clothes on the floor of my closet because all my drawers are full of my diaries.

So far, in this VCD group, we haven't had to talk. That probably comes later. Maybe soon. I try not to think about it.

So now I get to what Mr. O'Malley said. On the second Thursday—yesterday—after we'd got to know him a bit, he said, "I'm going to give you your main assignment. It's open-ended. The only requirement is that you have to fill one Hilroy exercise book by the time the March break rolls around. In it, you'll be talking about your most visible problem for thirty-two pages. *That will be your only subject matter.* You could cheat by writing big. Or you could fill your notebook with useless stuff. Like what you eat for breakfast or whether you like blonds better than redheads. *Don't do that.* This isn't a diary. This is *therapy.* If you don't know what that means, look it up in the dictionary."

Then he just stood there and looked at us for a few moments, as though he was waiting for all that to sink in. Next, he went over and stood beside a flip chart he keeps at the front of the room. The first thing he wrote on it was WHO I AM, in very big letters.

"But before you start your major assignment, write that down," he said, "and then get ready to describe yourself. Not just your problem. *Anything. Everything.* How old you are. What your family's like. If your family has just one parent or none, say so. If you're with a foster family, say so. If you hate spinach and love ice cream, say so. Here's your chance to tell me what you eat for breakfast and if you prefer blonds. Describe how tall you are, how handsome, how ugly, whether you wear glasses, who decides what clothes you wear, who likes you, who doesn't, what you do in your spare time. I'm not requiring you to talk yet, so I need some other way to get to know you."

Mr. O'Malley was silent for a moment. "Okay," he went on, "WHO I AM has to be done at home. I'd actually like to see it as soon as possible, so have it ready by next Thursday. I want at least three pages, single spaced."

Henry McLaughlin's eyes were wild. *"Hey!"* he actually shouted. *"You said 'the March break!'"* He looked ready to smash the desk with his fist, which was raised about six inches above it. His knuckles were shiny and white. His hand—the one holding his pencil—was trembling.

"I'm sorry, Henry," said Mr. O'Malley, and he looked as if he really meant it. "I guess I misled you. Absolutely my fault. The part that I'm about to discuss with you will be due by the start of March break—the real heavy-duty assignment. But I'd like to have everyone's WHO I AM in my hands by next Thursday. I apologize for not making that clear."

Henry was so stunned to hear an apology coming out of someone who was almost a teacher that his hand stopped shaking and his mouth flew open. Mr. O'Malley continued on without a pause, facing us, making eye contact.

"Okay," he said. "Now comes the hard part. Or maybe not. Time will tell." He went to the flip chart again and wrote down PROBLEM.

"What we need to do now," he said, "is to think about the sorts of things you'll be talking about in your big assignment." He walked back to his chair and sat down opposite our semicircle of five desks. He looked at all of us.

"You know by now," he said, "what your main problem is, so write it down. If you punched four people last week, your most *visible* problem is violence. Write that down. In the course of these sessions and of this assignment, you may discover some other problems that cause that behaviour. We'll deal with that later. For now, stick with the most obvious."

I could see Henry McLaughlin writing down ANGER. I wrote down FEAR. The principal was right about the gender thing. It would have been impossible for me to write that down so openly, so *nakedly,* if that blond and curly-haired Annika Setko had been sitting in one of those five chairs. Not, mind you, that Annika Setko could ever be a VCD.

I watched the other guys out of the corner of my eye. Of course, being me, I was scared to look at them head-on. There was a lot of pencil rubbing and nail biting. They seemed to be having trouble identifying their problems. I saw George Thornbloom write down a big V—and then cross it out. He chewed his lip for a bit, and then wrote down ANGER. Two Angers and one Fear, I thought. Then Jamieson

Freebury, who has almost no fingernails, wrote ANXIETY on his first page. Right afterwards, Donald Wilmington heaved a long, deep sigh and wrote the same thing. Having seen Donald in action, I expected to see him write ANGER or VIOLENCE (and certainly I was scared to death of him), but probably he decided that ANXIETY was safer. Which maybe, come to think of it, just shows how anxious he really is.

"Then," Mr. O'Malley said, "write down some of the things or people or experiences that make you *angry* or *fearful* or *anxious* or *violent*—that you think cause your problem. Make a list of those bits of information on the left hand side of the page under the title CAUSES, leaving a few spaces under each item.

"At the top of the right hand side of the page write WHY. Then write a reason opposite everything on your list. Let's just take one problem and do a sample."

He wrote on the flip chart

PROBLEM

ANGER

Causes	Why
Brother	Too bossy
Homework	Too hard
	Too much
Team sports	Kids say I'm no good
	Everyone plays rough
Frustration	I want everything
	to be easy
	I want to win
Mother	Scolds me all the time
	Hates my haircut
Other kids	Too stupid
	I don't like them
	They're sissies
Sister	Spends too long
	in the bathroom
	Makes fun of me

I could hardly wait to start. I wanted like anything to write this stuff down. I knew what the things were that scared me. And some of the time I thought I knew why. But not often. I was even scared to be in this group. Why? I didn't know. I was scared to answer questions in class, even when I knew the answers. Why? I didn't know. But I knew I'd probably be filling six of those Hilroy notebooks before March.

But suddenly I was looking at an enormous fear, a terrifying thought. It was making me walk on all those upturned nails. Here it was: *I needed to know if we'd have to let the other kids read our assignments, and I was scared to ask*. But I KNEW I'D BE TOO FRIGHTENED TO WRITE DOWN ONE SINGLE WORD UNLESS I KNEW THE ANSWER TO THAT QUESTION. Why? Because I was afraid of what those kids would do with that information.

That added up to two fears. Which was worse? To ask the question or not to know the answer? Both were scary. *But if I got rid of one, the other might go away*. I did a lot of fast and very serious thinking.

My pencil was rat-tat-tatting against my desk. My heart skipped a bunch of beats. I hoped I wasn't having a heart attack.

I shut my eyes and put up my hand. It was one of the hardest things I ever did. I mean it.

"Yes, Peter," said Mr. O'Malley's friendly voice.

I could just barely get it out. But even though I stuttered a lot and had to cough quite a few times, I did it. What I said was, "Will the other kids see the stuff we write?"

"No," said Mr. O'Malley. "They won't."

I had killed one fear with another fear.

It was like a miracle. The weight that lifted off my head, my shoulders, my chest was as heavy as a truckful of lumber. Without it, I felt, for a minute, lighter than air. I was also aware of something tickling my funnybone. Here is what I was thinking: *I'm in this room with two Anxieties and two Angers and a Shrink. What's more, one of the Anxieties is really a Violent. And right this second, none of them scares me. The real Anxiety may turn out to be a friend. His fingernails look exactly like mine. If I had a friend I'd feel safer. And I feel safe with Mr. O'Malley. Or almost safe. And maybe safe people are friends, even if they're the wrong age.*

Mr. O'Malley was going on and on about the assignment, but I was only listening with a small slice of my brain. However, I got the drift. Obviously we were going to be thinking about and deciphering our separate problems from now until March. This was a little bit frightening, but not very. After all, I felt like I'd been thinking about my fears ever since the minute I was born. I feel bad about that. As a matter of fact, I feel bad most of the time. But no one ever asked that big *WHY* before. And now Mr. O'Malley was saying something really interesting. He said that in our assignment we should also write down some of the things that could make our Problem less awful. Already I was listing them in my head:

— Cats, because they move slowly and gracefully and purr when you stroke them. Also, they seem to like me. They come up to me on the street and rub my leg. I wish I had a cat. They make me almost calm.

— Storms, with waves crashing and trees blowing around. They make me feel better about my own rage. Rage? So I must be an Anger, too. Some of the time, anyway. Yes. Yes, I am.

— Old Mr. Corkum on Preston Street. He talks to me about being in the Second World War, and tells me about how you can feel brave and terrified all at the same time. I understand that now, because of the brave thing I just did—even though most people would think that the brave thing I did today was smaller than nothing.

I found myself writing my WHO I AM homework before Mr. O'Malley had even stopped talking. "I'm Peter Jefferson," I wrote. "I'm fourteen years old, and I live in Halifax. I'm scared of just about every-thing—kids, grown-ups, most teachers, my father, my mother, my older brother, our huge dog, school, crowds, being alone, the dark, graveyards, traffic, sickness, dying. I'm scared most of the time. But for half an hour this afternoon I didn't feel any fear at all. That must mean something. I'm not sure what. But I'll tell you one thing—whatever it is, it's not something that I'm afraid of."

I was still writing after the other kids had left the class. I looked up at Mr. O'Malley, and we smiled at each other. Then I gathered up my books and backpack and left the room.

The Poem

Julia Parsons left the classroom, closing the door quietly. In fact, she closed it so softly that she could barely hear the small muffled click. She shut the door in this particular way because what she really wanted to do was slam it. She was very afraid that she might actually do that. In her head, or her heart, or possibly in the pit of her stomach, she was often afraid of what she might do if that tightly tied knot inside her started to unravel. Once, when her mother was going into one of her tailspins of criticism about the way Julia dressed (or cut her hair, or painted her toenails green, or went out with the wrong boyfriends, or had the wrong attitude), Julia had felt that rigid knot spring apart in one swift movement. It was during dinnertime, and the family was sitting at the table, faced with grim bowls of white tapioca. Without knowing she was doing it, Julia picked up a knife from her place setting. She *saw* herself pick it up. If she had had the wit to think about it, she would have known that in a bowl of tapioca there is nothing that needs to be cut. But there was no wit in operation at that moment, nor did she need to be told why she had picked up that knife, even though she hadn't *willed* herself to do it. With exaggerated care and deceptive calm, Julia lowered the knife and returned it to its position on the table. Then she excused herself from the meal. "Feel kind of sick," she mumbled, and went upstairs to lock herself in the bathroom. She sat on the edge of the bathtub with her hands tightly clasped, waiting for the trembling to stop.

Ever afterwards, whenever Julia was told about "a crime of passion," she felt she knew precisely what it was. She didn't condone it. She simply understood it.

But when Julia closed the door with such an inaudible click, she wasn't at home. She was standing in the corridor of her high school in Yarmouth, still holding tightly to the doorknob, wondering what to do with her anger. To right and to left, the mockingly cheerful orange lockers marched up and down the long hall, and the floors were still shining from the previous night's coat of wax. The floor was a mottled beige, more in keeping with her mood. As dull, Julia thought, as the English lesson from which she was escaping.

She started to move slowly along the corridor, and then walked down a hall in the direction of the wash-room. Then—much to her surprise—she turned completely around, re-entered the main corridor, and travelled left, passing another classroom and more lockers. And stepped out the front door of the school.

In all the sixteen years of her life, she had never once skipped school. Well, not quite. She didn't go to school if she was sick enough to have a temperature. Also, when her uncle was killed at a railway crossing and the funeral was on a Tuesday, of course she had to skip that one afternoon and go to the funeral. But she attended school in the morning. What if she'd been overcome with grief? Would her family have insisted that she take only the afternoon off? But no one in the family seemed to be overcome with grief. "Silly damn fool," she had heard her father say on Sunday morning, after the phone call had come. "Trying to race the train."

Her mother had been dry-eyed ever since the news had come. "He's been playing games with death as long as I can remember," she said that night over the Sunday chicken. "Competitive games. Competing with the long sleep. Or the rest of his life in a wheelchair. Like the time Johnny MacIntosh dared him to leap across that wide chasm in the rocks at Peggy's Cove, when they were both ten. Or when he first got his ATV two years ago, the way he'd cross his fingers and drive it across the thin ice of Lake Annis in April—just for the hell of it. And him with a wife and four kids." Her whole body was rigid with exasperation. Even her grammar was out of whack. It wasn't like her to slip up in that area. And *him* with a wife and four kids.

Then she continued. "But he always won that game. That game with death. Guess he thought his lucky star would always protect him. Until this morning." She put her napkin on the table and pushed her plate away. "It makes me so mad!" she whispered, adding, "And it always did." *Mad,* not angry. She *was* upset. Forgetting for a few minutes to keep her background under wraps.

So—one afternoon off for that funeral. And everyone dry-eyed. But quite a few people looking angry. *It's an angry family,* Julia had thought at the time, *but Mom's the only one who's allowed to let it all out. The rest of us have to keep our mad stuff squashed down inside.*

And that's why Julia had closed the door softly when she'd left the classroom. She thought about that later, as she walked down Main Street in the direction of the road to the Bar Harbour ferry. She'd maybe go down to the terminal and watch the Americans pouring off "The Cat," and hope that her mother hadn't chosen today to go shopping. Not a chance. It was Monday—washday. Mrs. Parsons wasn't one to decide to postpone doing laundry just because there weren't enough dirty clothes in the hamper. She'd scuttle around the house picking up any old bits and pieces of clothing, washing *clean* things rather than switch her washday to Tuesday. *Inflexible,* thought Julia. *Oh, let me be loose and easy to live with when I get to be as old as Mom.*

Julia reached in her pocket, and could tell by the feel of the coins that she had several quarters in there. She ran her thumbnail along their edges to make sure they weren't nickels. *A Coke would help,* she thought, and turned in to a small convenience store that had a narrow counter at the back, with six high stools. People often dropped in there during their break, for a cup of coffee or a Pepsi or maybe just a chocolate chip cookie. Well, she was on her break. Walking past the rows of cough drops, bubble gum, and chocolate bars, past the packages of microwave popcorn, tired-looking apples, and spotted bananas, Julia headed for the counter. All the stools were empty. Good. It was nine forty-five—still early. People could be nosy and ask questions; so those vacant seats looked perfect.

Adrianna Johnson was behind the counter, dressed in an almost-white cotton apron—heavy cotton, like in an old-fashioned canvas potato bag. Julia remembered one of those from her grandmother's house. She kept old jam jars in it. Adrianna was measuring coffee into a filter cup. She had something that looked like a shower cap on her head, from which a few corkscrew curls of ginger-coloured hair were escaping onto her forehead.

"Hi, Adrianna," said Julia, and sat down. Adrianna had been in her class last year—in Grade 10—but had left suddenly, in the middle of the year. Julia hadn't known her well; they didn't hang out with the same kids. But if you're skipping school for the very first time since Grade 1, it's nice to run across someone who isn't a parent or a neighbour or a teacher's spouse. "How's it going?" she said.

Adrianna didn't answer Julia's question. She raised her eyes from the coffee pot and looked hard at Julia. "You're not in school," she said.

"No," said Julia.

"Dropped out?"

"No. Just walked out." They were all alone, and Adrianna was the same age. Maybe it'd be okay to talk about it. "Just walked out," she repeated, "because I couldn't stand to be in the same room as Miss Holloway for two more seconds."

"Ah, yes," said Adrianna. "New teacher last year. But old. Maybe fifty. Thought she knew every goddamn thing. Acted like we was all born without brains." Adrianna's thin face broke into a grin. "You just *walked out?* I thought you was an apple polisher."

An apple polisher. So that's what her mother had made her into.

"Not *her* apple." Julia found herself laughing.

"Are you goin' back?"

"Oh, sure," sighed Julia. "She thinks I'm in the washroom. I didn't go throwing erasers or kicking my desk or anything. I just *went.* She probably won't even notice that I didn't come back."

Adrianna didn't speak for a few moments. She placed the coffee and filter in the machine, poured a full pot of water in the opening, placed the pot on its burner, and pressed the On button.

"They'll all start pilin' into here in about fifteen minutes," said Adrianna, "and when they do, they want their coffee *now*. If I'm lookin' for tips, I better be ready." Then she came over and leaned her elbows on the counter. "I want to tell you something," she said.

"Like what?"

"Like when I was still in school, I never liked you."

Julia felt a familiar pushing sensation in the general area of her diaphragm. It was what she felt when her mother started telling her all the ways in which Julia had failed her as a daughter. *This is not my day,* she thought. She flipped her long brown hair over her shoulder to show that she didn't care. Be damned if she was going to let Adrianna Johnson squash her flat. Who did she think *she* was? Julia had heard stories about her father. And they lived in that awful box of a house that hadn't been painted in fifty million years.

"And that, too," said Adrianna. "It bugged the hell out o' me when you did that."

"Did *what?*"

"That flippin' thing with your hair. Even without the flippin', it was hard to like anyone who had hair like yours. Everyone knows that if you have curly hair, you hate it. You want it to be long and straight and shiny, like you got. Like in the TV ads. Some gorgeous doll comes sailin' onto the set in her three-inch heels, and her hair is swingin' from side t' side like a sheet in the wind. You seen it a hundred times. Then she holds up a bottle o' the shampoo she uses. Instant beauty. You gotta laugh."

Julia found it hard to ask the next question. But she'd walked out of English class this morning. The thought of it made her feel … *what?* She tried to find words for the way she felt. *I feel released. I've done one weird thing. Maybe I can do another.*

"What else didn't you like about me?"

Adrianna grinned. "Don't lose no sleep over it. It was mostly that you come from the snotty side o' town and got good marks. And I didn't. I skipped school a lot, so my marks got bad. And look where you *live*. It didn't make me love you t' know that. You know where *my* house is."

Yes, I do. It's three doors away from the place where my mother was born.

"What else? Anything else?"

"Well … you did seem kind of a nerd. I kept hopin' you'd do something wrong or bad. *Anything* woulda done. You was just way too perfect."

Then Adrianna reached across the counter and gave Julia's hand a small pat. "And now you done it," she said. "So it's like someone just gave me permission t' like you."

Suddenly Julia felt warm from her big toe to the top of her head. Not hot. *Warm*—the way you'd feel on a very cold day when someone had just given you a soft wool sweater to put on.

"How do you *do* that?" she asked Adrianna.

"Do what?"

"Just up and tell someone you don't like them. Or *didn't* like them. I'd never have the guts to do that."

Adrianna laughed as she ran a damp cloth over the countertop. "If we didn't do that in our family, we'd get ploughed right under. Us kids always tell it like it is. There are seven of us."

"Seven!"

"Yeah. Seven."

"You talk to your parents like that too?"

"You kiddin'? Pa'd beat us up if we did. And he's some big."

"*Beat* you?"

"Yeah. You heard me right."

Julia stared at the coffee pot and thought about that. But Adrianna spoke first.

"Why'd you walk out o' class? What'd old lady Holloway do t' make you that riled up?"

Julia sighed again. She knew this was going to sound silly. Adrianna would start hating her again. But just thinking about it made her mad enough to forget all that.

"Because she was wrecking a poem." There. She'd said it.

Adrianna stared at her for a long moment. Then she repeated Julia's words.

"*Because she was wrecking a poem.* Gimme a break, Julia."

"Yeah. Okay. But not just any old poem. One of my favourite ones. It's by Keats. It's called 'On First Looking into Chapman's Homer.' It's so beautiful that when I read it, I want to just lie down and die."

"Die, eh? Gotta be strong stuff. How does it go?"

Julia took a deep breath.

"It starts, *'Much have I travell'd in the realms of gold.'* Doesn't that almost make your heart turn over?"

"Well, no. But I don't have a heart that turns over all that easy. Still, when you say it, it does sound … well, y' know, okay. How did she wreck it?"

"She never once read it right through. If she had, I might be able to forgive her. But no such luck. She *started* by going through it line by line, word by word—like a grocery list, for God's sake. In that first line she went on and on about *realms*—what they were, how to define the word, and why old Keats chose to use it. Then she went the same route with *gold.* Did she have to tear *that* word apart and give it ten different meanings?"

Julia put her elbows on the counter and leaned her forehead on both hands. "It might even have been interesting," she said, "if she'd done that line-by-line thing *later.* Maybe it could even help kids to understand the poem. But she didn't *once* let us hear the *whole thing.* Adrianna, can I have a Coke, please?"

Adrianna passed her over a glass and filled it. "Then what?" she said.

Julia took a long sip from the straw. "Well," she began, "When she got to the line that says, *'Till I heard Chapman speak out loud and bold,'* do you think she could let that one go by? Huh! We had to have a whole biography and bibliography of Mr. Chapman and how he got tangled up with Homer. And of course before we ever got back to the poem, she told us more than anyone would ever want to know about Homer, and just about everything the guy ever wrote."

"Yeah. Boring. Sounds boring."

"Boring! *Yes!* But listen!" Julia put down her Coke and actually stood up. She spoke slowly and softly:

> *Then felt I like some watcher of the skies*
> *When a new planet swims into his ken;*
> *Or like stout Cortez, when with eagle eyes*
> *He stared at the Pacific—and all his men*
> *Look'd at each other with a wild surmise—*
> *Silent, upon a peak in Darien.*

Adrianna frowned. "Nice," she said. "When you say it, when you *speak* it, I gotta admit … it sounds some nice." She was polishing a glass over and over and over. "And?"

"And she took that planet," said Julia savagely, "and gave us a whole astronomy lesson. And of course with *'stout Cortez,'* we got practically the whole history of Spain. *She killed the poem.* She *killed* it. It was like seeing my best friend run over by a truck. And I had to just sit there and watch it happen." She looked at Adrianna and screwed up her eyebrows. "What'll I do, Adrianna?"

Adrianna smiled. "I dunno, Julia," she said, "but you're not so big a wimp as I thought you was. You could try *tellin'* her." Julia was shaking her head. "Or, if you can't hack that, you could come in for a Coke once in a while and tell *me.* That 'eagle eyes' part was kinda cool. I'd listen. Honest."

Then Adrianna went on, "Julia, I didn't wanta quit school, but Pa made me. He needed money t' feed that army o' kids. He says if he has that many horses, he got t' harness some o' them. My brother, Joe—he only just turned fifteen—is workin' on a trawler already." She looked up and focused on the doorway. Past the spotted bananas and microwave popcorn and cough drops and chocolate bars, four men were moving in their direction.

"Break time," said Adrianna. "No more poems this morning. But come back sometime. I like the sound of it when you do that poetry stuff out loud. And you can tell me about it when you're mad at Miss Holloway, in case you can't tell *her*. You can fill me in about the kids, too. I sure miss hangin' out with them."

Julia noticed that people were smiling at her as she walked back up Main Street. *Why?* Then she realized that she was walking along with a smile on her own face. She'd missed seeing the ferry, but she didn't care. Anyway, she'd better get moving. If she hurried, she could make it back to school in time for math class. She knew she'd never be able to tell Miss Holloway that she wrecked the poetry she was trying so hard to teach. But maybe, just maybe, she could ask her mother—nicely, but firmly—to try not to criticize every single thing she wore and did and *was*. It might be possible. Then again it might not. In any case, Adrianna seemed to be really good at listening. Julia could see that she might be drinking a lot of Coke this spring.

Father by Mail

Dear Dad,

Ever since you and Mom broke up, I've got to know you better. I bet that seems strange to you. After all, you're not around any more. I don't even know why you left. I often wonder if you went because you wanted to go, or if Mom asked you to leave. She doesn't talk about it now, and she never did, even right at the beginning. Also, she never said any bad stuff about you—then or now. What's more, you never mention it when me and Lisa go to Sydney for those very long weekends. And of course (me and her, she and I, the two of us) never discuss it. First off, she's a girl, and worse still, she's three years older than me. It's like she lives in another world.

When you left, Lisa was sixteen, and thought she was twenty. She went around with this closed-up look on her face. I thought it was an I've-got-a-secret kind of look, and it scared the pants off me. I figured she knew why you left, but if so, her lips were sealed with contact cement or Crazy Glue. I was thirteen and a boy—her kid brother—the wrong age and the wrong sex. No way was she going to tell me anything, and no way was I brave enough to ask. Besides, I think that a very large chunk of me didn't really want to know. By now, I figure Lisa never knew anything anyway. She was just trying to act omniscient.

You maybe wonder why I'm choosing now to bring up all that ancient history. It's because I turned sixteen yesterday—the same age Lisa was when you left—and I'm as full of unanswered questions as I ever was. If you feel an uncontrollable urge to tell me anything, feel free. I'm listening.

But even if you don't, I still know you better in our letters than I ever knew you when you lived at

1625 Poplar Street. You were never *there*. You left for work when we were all rushing around getting ready for school—looking for matching socks, fighting about who got to use the bathroom, burning the toast. Not a time for warm and intimate conversations, as you streaked out of the house with your briefcase, often without even saying Goodbye or See you later. Mom would be feverishly searching for the missing sock, running referee outside the bathroom, making more toast. By the time you got home, we were all through supper and doing homework. Later on, you'd shut yourself in your study and work some more, or maybe go back to the office—or wherever it was you went.

Once I went down to the kitchen at eleven forty-five at night to get a glass of water. My throat was dry and scratchy, and I felt awful. Mom was sitting at the table with her hands in her lap, just staring at the stove on the other side of the room. The room was silent except for the ticking clock and the humming refrigerator. She was surrounded by dirty dishes—with all the yucky food dried on them—and pots and pans and a carafe of cold coffee. I remember that scene like it was yesterday, but I didn't even speak to her. A very small section of my brain may have wondered why she hadn't got rid of all that mess— after all, it was close to midnight—but I was eleven years old and feeling sorry for myself. I just hauled a clean glass out of the cupboard and filled it with water.

She finally jolted herself out of her stupor and said, "You okay?"

"No," I said. "I got a bad sore throat and my head aches. And I'm freezing cold. I feel like I'm gonna die in the next five minutes."

That did it. She sprang into action, and first thing I knew I was back in bed with a heating pad and Granny's old comforter and an aspirin and hot lemonade. Later, I heard the clattering of dishes in the kitchen.

This is a long letter, but being as I just turned sixteen—which is a *significant birthday*, even if you did forget it—I thought I'd stop pushing everything down inside and start *expressing* myself.

But I also wanted to say that I like getting letters from you. It's only once a month, and on precisely the same day, but man, oh man, that sure beats hearing absolutely nothing. We didn't even used to meet up in the bathroom, because you and Mom had one of your own.

How come you write on the exact same day? Does that secretary of yours leave a note on your desk that says, "October 1. Write Patrick"? Or do you have some sort of gadget like Mom's kitchen timer—the one that's red, and shaped like a red pepper—that counts out days instead of minutes? On the first day of the month it yells "Bing!" and you drop all your court cases and litigations and torts, and pick up your pen. One page exactly, 8½ by 11, mailed in a business-sized envelope with the name of your law firm up in the corner (Black, Simcoe, and MacDonald). One for me. One for Lisa. One for Mom, but hers has a cheque in it. As regular and predictable as the dawn, those three envelopes come rolling in on the third day of every month. Sometime I'd really like to get one in the middle of the month, so that I could kid myself that you'd sent it just because you were thinking about me, and had kind of an itch to say Hello, Patrick. But the first-day-of-the-month letter is still better than the old days. I get to hear *something* from you, and then I get to send my own news back. I tell myself that you're listening. Are you?

This letter is too long. I'm supposed to be mowing the lawn.

Your son,

Patrick

September 4

Dear Dad,

Tonight I'm not going to talk about your leaving. That's old stuff. I want to talk about my own life, so maybe you can answer me if I have any questions.

Here's what we're all doing right now. Mom has a job selling ... guess what? Cars. Volvos. One week she may make a bundle and we go out to Harvey's or Swiss Chalet *twice*. The next week she may sell nothing, and we're back to Kraft Dinner and wieners again. She took a course in it, and had to learn about the cars' guts as well as their skins. She came first in her class and was so proud of herself that we thought she might burst. I coughed up some of my paper route money and Lisa added a bunch from her weekend job at Lawtons. We bought her three sunflowers (her favourite, in case you happen not to remember) and a big chocolate layer cake with pink frosting and a picture of a Volvo on it, drawn in blue icing. Underneath it said, "CONGRATULATIONS!"

Lisa is at university, taking psychology and piling up her debt. She says she hopes her course will help her understand her weird family. She wants to be a clinical psychologist. She's going to Dalhousie, so she still lives at home. She's okay. I almost like her, even though she acts like I'm mentally challenged and like she's Einstein's favourite sister. She's nineteen and has a boyfriend who's taking law, which I told her is a big mistake, because lawyers work all the time and haven't got five minutes a day to spend with their families. But all she did was make a snorting noise and say, "Get lost, Patrick." She may be smart, but apparently she has no memory. (Apologies, Dad.)

I'm in Grade 11. It's the most brutal class in the school. It's full of students who act like they want to kill each other. But I have a best friend, so I feel safe from bullies and kids who try to push me around. A best friend performs that excellent function. I've noticed this, and I watch people a lot. If a kid has a best friend, bullies mostly leave him alone, because fighting one person can mean fighting two, and bullies like things to be easier than that. They're basically lazy. They don't want to make either friends or enemies the hard way.

My friend's name is Chuck, and he was my best friend from way back when you more or less lived with us. (I realize that was another cheap shot, but Lisa says we need to take out our past resentments and look at them, and maybe *express* them from time to time. That one just sort of came out, so I left it sitting on the page, hoping it could be what Lisa keeps calling "a healthy form of self-expression.")

I also have a girlfriend called Caroline Ryan, who I like a lot. She's quiet and sort of shy, and has short tangled-looking curly hair and is quite skinny and small, with cute little half-orange breasts. Large Florida oranges, not the tiny Sunkist kind. She gets along fine with Mom and Lisa, even though Lisa is so sort of *in charge*. Caroline has a whole complete family with a mother, a father, and twin brothers. I go over there a lot. Most mothers have jobs, but Mrs. Ryan doesn't. She tries to be home when the twins (Grade 4—a pair of afterthoughts) come home from school, just like Mom used to. The kitchen is a warm and friendly place, and you can often smell things cooking. She uses a lot of cinnamon. Even chocolate. Talk about heaven.

This is another long letter. I'm realizing that I never told you much about myself in the letters I sent to you before. Now I want you to know who your son is.

How about you telling me something about *you*? I guess I can't expect you to tell me why you left, but it would be good to hear something that would make you seem more real to me. Even little things. Like do you ever go to a movie? If so, which ones do you like? What books do you enjoy? Or do you just read *The Law Review*? What foods turn you on?

Do you drink beer or wine or the hard stuff or all of the above—or none? Do you have a girlfriend, or are you too old for all that stuff? Do you get any exercise? I play soccer and walk six of the neighbours' dogs. I love animals a lot. Maybe better than people.

Your son,

Patrick

October 5

Dear Dad,

I got your monthly letter, which arrived on October 3. Thank you for answering some of my questions. I like quiche and caesar salad too, so let's have it the next time I go to Sydney. But let's also have some fries. And maybe steak on one of the nights. I told Lisa you like historical novels, and she was pleased because she enjoys them, too, even though I don't. But I like some novels, just so long as there's lots of lovemaking going on, with maybe some murder or war thrown in to keep things moving along. And I like any book about animals. I don't really think you're too old to have a girlfriend. But if you work all day and night like you used to, probably you can't fit one into your schedule. Women and girls (even Caroline, for instance) like to have *something* happening once in a while—like a movie or a day at the beach (in summer), or an event that makes them feel special or sort of *cherished*. I expect you have to eat from time to time, so you could take a beautiful middle-aged widow out to a classy restaurant and eat quiche and caesar salad and have some of that red wine you like.

Why is it easier to talk to you on paper than with my voice? When Lisa and I go to Sydney for those very long weekends, it seems to me we always wind up watching documentaries on TV because no one can think of anything to say.

Chuck is okay with me spending a lot of time with Caroline. But he doesn't want me to hang out with other guys. It's like he thinks he owns me. But I'd like to have more than just one friend. It's more *interesting*. Chuck has a girlfriend, but she's kind of wild and does a lot of drugs and stuff—particularly *stuff*—so Caroline and I don't spend much time with them. I may be sort of growing away from Chuck, because all he seems to think about is sex and drinking, and that's okay for *some* of the time but not *all* the time. But Chuck doesn't just want to *do* it all the time. He wants to *talk* about it all the time. There are other topics in the world.

Mom has a boyfriend. They go to movies and sometimes out to dinner. I don't know what else they do, and I'm not sure I want to think about it. It's hard to imagine parents being anything except parents. This guy's name is Henry. He's okay. I can take him or leave him. But I don't want him to move in and start trying to act like a father. Lisa says not to be stupid, because in a couple of years I'll be out of here, anyway. I want to go to the Atlantic Veterinarian College in Charlottetown. It's the only thing I want to do, so Caroline says if I go there, she'll go to UPEI and get her nursing degree from them instead of Dal. Dal would be cheaper because I could live at home, but they don't train vets. But I already have summer jobs with the SPCA lined up here, and have worked there part-time since I was fourteen. I also walk dogs for money (did I say that before?), and look after people's cats and birds when they go on trips. So I figure I'll be more or less okay.

All for now. Feel free to comment on my opinions about friendships.

Your son,

Patrick

November 6

Dear Dad,

I'm glad you agree it's a good idea to have more than just one friend. Chuck's family is thinking of moving out west. If your best friend moves from Nova Scotia to Calgary and drops you like a hot potato—and doesn't ever write to you—it can be pretty rough. I know Chuck just would *not* write letters, even once a month on a designated day. So that would be that. I'd be right back in the midst of that murderous bunch of Grade 11 thugs, with no one to talk to except Caroline. And she's on the gymnastics team and sometimes does other girl stuff.

A guy keeps talking to me in the cafeteria when I'm alone—when Chuck's doing detentions or Caroline's home sick—and he's got lots to say. His name is Andrew. He talks about disembodied stuff like books we've both read or music he likes, as well as his three cats and two dogs. We have no animals—as you may or may not remember—because Lisa is allergic to anything with four legs or wings. This guy has a couple of friends, but that doesn't stop the bullies from tripping him in the hall or making fun of the way he walks. He's more interesting than Chuck, but Chuck'd be mad if I spent time with him—*any* time. And I'll admit that I'm scared of how the bullies will treat me if I attach myself to a potential Victim.

Do you have any opinions on what I should do? Lisa and I don't bother Mom with our problems. We've tried to make things easier for her ever since you took flight. Lisa says to do what I want, that I'm not Chuck's slave. But she doesn't know what bullies can do. She's always been so fierce and tough that a bully would have to be a Goliath before he'd try to attack her.

Your son,

Patrick

November 18

Dear Dad,

I'm waiting for your answer to my question. Maybe you could force yourself to write a letter in the middle of the month. Don't you even *like* me and Lisa? Is your writing hand paralyzed or something? I've tried not to feel mad at you about your sudden disappearance. But now I got to tell you that I feel a rolling bubble rising in me—the kind that precedes a volcanic eruption, which then pours forth sputtering lava before it lets loose with a river of red death. Red is an angry colour.

Your son, I guess,

Patrick

November 24

Dear Dad,

I damn near died when I got your letter on November 23rd. If you want to know what I did, here it is. I went in the bathroom, turned on the shower, and cried. I cried a long time, and when I'd finished, the hot water was used up, the walls and ceiling were audibly dripping, and Lisa was banging on the door. I left the room with a towel over my head, like I'd been washing my hair. I didn't want anyone to see my puffy eyes. After all, I'm sixteen.

Then I went into my bedroom and read your letter again. You apologized for being an absentee father. I couldn't believe my eyes. You said not to feel trapped by my friendship with Chuck if all he wants to do is drink, do drugs, and sleep around. You said that when you left, it wasn't Mom's fault. There it was, one 8½ by 11 page in the middle of a month. But it was like a miracle. No wonder I cried. Lisa once told me that it's perfectly all right for grown *men* to cry, and that what's more, it would be good for them to do it more often. Sometimes Lisa knows what she's talking about.

Thanks, Dad.

Patrick

P.S. Enclosed is my school photo.

December 4

Dear Dad,

New problem. Chuck says that Andrew is gay. He says that if I start being friendly with him, everyone will think I'm gay, too. He also says that he, Chuck, will permanently terminate his friendship with me if I start talking to Andrew in the cafeteria or walking home from school with him. (We live on the same street.) He says the bullies are mean to Andrew because they know he's gay. Yesterday he said, "Watch out, or it'll be like wearing a permanent tattoo that says, 'I'm gay too.'"

This is a big mess, Dad. I like Andrew and don't care a shit if he's gay. What's so bad about being gay? It's gotta be some screw-up in your hormonal system, and you're *born* that way. Andrew isn't making *advances* to me. He just wants to talk about animals and music. And so do I. Why are people so mean? Why do they *care* if Andrew is gay or not? Why? Why? Why? It's none of their *business*.

But I got to admit, Dad, that I'm scared. I don't want people thinking I'm gay just because I talk to Andrew once in a while. I don't want Chuck to abandon me, either.

Lisa says to just thumb my nose at the bunch of them and do what I want. Caroline says she's a protection for me because everyone knows we're in love. I gave her a ring last week—just a little silver ring with a fake stone in it. It only cost seven dollars, but man, oh man, does she love that ring! I feel like I want to marry her right *now*, so that I won't have to worry about bullies tripping me in the hall or calling me a fag, or losing Chuck's peculiar friendship, or being cut off from all the nice guys out there who might be gay. I bet the school is full of them, scared to move, hiding in the closet.

Help me, Dad. What'll I do?

Patrick

December 14

Dear Dad,

I was almost knocked unconscious by your letter. I was so relieved and stunned and amazed that I did the crying-in-the-bathroom thing again. It seems like things are opening up for me so fast that I almost can't handle it.

Now, at last, I understand so much, all in one thundering swoop. All your obsessive work and late nights away; Mom sitting among the dirty dishes at midnight, staring at the stove; why you left, and why you didn't explain anything to us. At thirteen, I sure wouldn't have understood. But I bet Lisa would have taken it all in her stride if she'd been told. But maybe not. And now I see why Mom wasn't mad. There was nothing to be *mad at*. It all just *was*. Nobody's fault.

Mind you, those monthly letters were almost an insult, in spite of being better than nothing. But even though you felt you couldn't tell me and Lisa you were gay, you could have shown more interest in *us*. We're your *children*. But you say that you thought it was the kindest thing to do to just disappear out of our lives. Well, it wasn't. We don't care if you're gay, and Lisa and I are even glad you have a nice partner called Morley, and that he cooks a mean steak and can even do French fries. So the next time we go to Sydney, don't evict him out of the apartment. Let's all be in the same place and get to know each other.

This also makes me feel better about Mom and Henry. It's okay if he moves in. I can see now that he doesn't want to be my father any more than I want to be his son. Besides, like Lisa says, we're both birds that will have flown from the nest before very long.

It's not going to be the easiest thing in the world, but I'm going to go on talking about books and music and animals with Andrew in the cafeteria and on the way home. You can't believe how much he knows about primates and the cat family. I'll let Chuck go, if he has to, but Caroline will stick by me, and I have a funny feeling that it'll all be more or less okay. Not perfect. But okay. Lisa says I'll end up feeling *empowered,* because I'll have had the guts—even wobbly guts—to move in my own direction. A while back, I said to you that I almost liked Lisa. I like her a lot now. She's on my side. And yours. And Mom's. Maybe we're not such a weird family after all.

Love,

Your son,

Patrick

P.S. Keep writing.

P.P.S. Hi to Morley.

Lillian

Her name is Lillian. She doesn't like her name, but this doesn't matter to her any more. Like so many other things—now that she is sixty-eight years old—her feelings about her name have lost their edge. This is not to say that she no longer has feelings. She has many emotions, and some of them are stronger than they ever were. Faced with certain appalling information or experiences of injustice, she can feel anger as debilitating and corrosive as it was when she was sixteen. But a lot of her reactions seem to have been softened or diluted by the passage of time. Possibly she's saved the intensity of her responses for the matters that are of the deepest concern to her.

Maybe she just doesn't have the requisite energy for all those other peripheral reactions. Who can say? But sometimes at night when she is unable to sleep—when attacked by the insomnia that seems to plague her more and more often of late—she lies there and thinks about other times and other places. It is then that memories of her childhood can comfort and calm her into a return to sleep, or else rise in her throat to choke her.

Tonight, for instance, she can tell from a vague sensation inhabiting her head that she may not find sleep until she starts to see the light creeping along the edge of her window blinds. She doesn't know how she knows this, but she does. She will be awake, eyes open, thinking. Lillian pictures her brain as a collection of multiple tidy compartments, holding memories, plans, knowledge of every kind, sensations, anxieties. Even the anxieties are neatly stacked, the contents of those compartments recognized and explicable. There are pigeonholes, for instance, for specific worries about her totally grown up children. She fears for their safety as urgently as she did when they were preschoolers. It is true that she doesn't examine those brain compartments as often as she did when they were small and defenceless and terrifyingly careless. But she can still centre on one of those familiar anxieties with a fear so intense as to make her cry out at its haunting clarity. She can imagine death and mutilation and every sort of danger and violation. When she is ninety-five, her son and daughter will be sixty and sixty-five. Lillian knows that if one of them dies at that time—dies before she does—her grief will consume her as savagely as if she were forty and they were five and ten years old.

But not all contents of her brain's compartments are always as accessible or as vividly examined. Certain past memories, although still there, seldom invite her scrutiny. She can pass over old embarrassments, betrayals, rude surprises, as though scanning the merchandise of a store that doesn't interest her— like, for instance, a hardware store. Screwdrivers, auto accessories, flashlights, bicycle pumps, extension cords: who cares? Usually, that's what it's like. She can see those memories, but they have ceased to concern her. And when sleep is near at hand, the compartments become blurry. All those sensations and memories and stray pieces of knowledge may slide along in view of her mind's eye, but markedly undefined.

Tonight, however, the pigeonholes are in focus and clear. Maybe that's how she knows that sleep will be slow in coming. That and the odd quality of the night. The moon is full, and the sky almost devoid of clouds. But those that are there are racing across the sky as though pursued by evil spirits. On this so-perfect night, a wild wind is blowing—slamming against the house and rattling the windows. The surf can be heard—a muffled roar—pounding on the cliffs of Granite Point, two miles away. No wonder she's so wakeful. No wonder the compartments and their contents are so graphic, so vivid.

Lillian is surfing her brain. She's doing it quickly, turning up a worry here, a fact there, a recent news item (an earthquake on a small Pacific island—occupying its own tiny space, sandwiched between the news of Jane Dorey's new baby and Lillian's recipe for a quick tuna casserole). She's skimming across memories now—the time Harriet Pritchard threw up all over Lillian's desk in Grade 3—all over her beautiful drawing of Noah's ark, splattering all the animals who were entering the ark two by two. There they all were—covered with Harriet's breakfast. Everyone was standing up, even the people on the far aisle by the window—wanting to avoid the dribbling mess, trying to see better, hoping to be properly horrified.

Next, Lillian is staring at another scene. She's watching Alexander Lovet on the day he started up the stairs to the stage in the assembly room, on the day of Grade 9 graduation. The principal had just announced that Alexander had won the prize for Athlete of the Year—the prize that Lillian had been hoping and hoping she would win. But no. It was Alexander's. As he reached the top step, he tripped and fell right onto the floor in front of the vice-principal. He scrambled to his feet, face scarlet with shame, his triumph wrecked by his humiliation. Lillian had to keep firm control of her facial muscles to prevent herself from smiling. She didn't want to admit, even to herself, how pleased she was. An athlete should never trip.

Lillian feels uncomfortable with that memory, but she lets it pass. She's on to the next scene. This time she's in Grade 11, in Queen Elizabeth High School. She wonders if this whole area of her brain is reserved for school memories. Even at age sixty-eight, Lillian has no idea how the brain really works. All she knows is the way it works for her.

Now Lillian is deeply into past tense, firmly engaged. She's not going to slide right out of this memory into another one. She'll stick around to look at all sides of it.

In Grade 11, Lillian was smart, but she was also lazy. Besides, there were a lot of things going on that interested her more than some of the subjects she was supposed to be studying. She was editor of the school yearbook, class president, and the best forward on the basketball team. Those things all took time. Sometimes she couldn't be bothered doing a good job on her homework. Her geography assignments, for instance.

That year, Miss Hackett was their geography teacher. She also taught them history and English. She could make those two subjects pretty pleasant, sometimes even exciting. But geography was a bummer. This was odd, because one of Lillian's daydreams was to be a world traveller—hiking through Europe with a knapsack on her back, or skiing across Siberia, the sky alive with northern lights. But geography just seemed to be a lot of boring memory work: Mexico: coastline 9,330 miles; climate mild to hot; products silver and cotton and rice; population 23,000,000. Or Switzerland: capital city Bern; languages German, French, Italian; government federal republic. Lillian always did her geography homework as quickly as possible in order to get it all over with. She knew that she often turned in messy projects, and her marks were consistently low. She didn't care. She'd long ago stopped trying to place first all the time.

But Lillian knew that she couldn't escape Miss Hackett's frown forever. This morning, after class, Miss Hackett (the Hatchet) had told her that she was hurt and disappointed as well as angry. "Lillian," she said, her brows squeezed together, "you ought to be *ashamed* of yourself. You were born with a good brain—something that doesn't happen to everyone. And you don't use it to its full capacity. I can't *stand* that. I can't tolerate the waste. I'm *disgusted*. If you don't pull up your socks and improve your work, I'm going to recommend to the principal that you stay after school and redo all your homework assignments for the past six weeks. I mean it."

Six weeks! She'd miss basketball practice, class meetings, work on the yearbook. She'd also get behind in her *other* homework. Lillian shot Miss Hackett a look full of hate, and stormed out of the classroom. *She'd show her!*

Lillian walked home through the drizzly afternoon. It was mid-November, and most of the leaves had fallen. The sidewalk was full of them—not crisp and cheerful to scrunch through or kick around. Just soggy and sometimes slippery, with all the lively fall colours leached out of them. To her left, Citadel Hill rose, dark and gloomy, its greenness faded to a dispiriting beige. A week of rain and wind had stripped the city of its optimism. The bare branches of the trees, the chill in the air, Camp Hill Cemetery—empty of flowers or visitors—all combined to drag down Lillian's spirits. Even the brightly coloured houses of Robie Street looked grey and despondent through the curtain of mist and fine rain.

When Lillian reached home, she dumped her coat in the front porch and stomped upstairs to her room to lick her wounds. She allowed herself ten minutes for concentrated self-pity. She liked Miss Hackett more than most of the other kids did, but she knew that she was capable of lowering a very heavy boom. Lillian both admired this quality and feared it. She could see that she was doomed to several days of concentrated geography. Her next assignment—the most important of the term—was due on Thursday, and this was Monday. She had known about it for three weeks, but she hadn't even opened her atlas. However, this time it had to be perfect. It had to be wonderful enough to make up for the last six weeks of sloppy work. Lillian hauled her geography text out of her book bag. She sat down on her bed and attacked the required chapter with what Miss Hackett called her good brain. She knew that a perfect assignment wouldn't be enough. She needed to *know* the material. When questions were asked in class, she had to be ready with accurate answers.

This week, the country was Brazil. She memorized information about location and boundaries, rainfall, crops, population, coastline, language, industries. By five o'clock she knew it all. She hadn't even heard her mother call out to her when she'd returned from shopping. She'd successfully crammed the whole long chapter, and it was firmly imbedded in her memory. She was an authority on Brazil. She could lead a group of tourists on a trip down the Amazon, spouting facts and figures, describing the flora and fauna of the areas they were passing through, serving indigenous foods for their elegant lunch, casually tossing out information about Brazilian culture, politics, climate, as the passengers sampled fried sweet potatoes, manioc meal, baked pineapple *(abacaxi assado)*, coconut milk. Lillian was already there. She smiled. She was ready for any class question that Miss

Hackett might ask. But now she was faced with the written part of the assignment, the major term essay.

For two days, Lillian spent every free minute on her assignment. This involved staying up until two each night. She skipped basketball practice, much to the consternation of her coach. She said she was ill with a complicated virus—well enough to attend school, but requiring rest the minute the academic day was over. Lying didn't come easily to Lillian, but she managed that one. After all, wasn't she doing this work in order to make sure she could attend all future practices? She'd heard the expression "The end justifies the means." She didn't know if people were supposed to agree with that or not. As a matter of fact, she wasn't dead sure if she knew what it really meant. Still, the gist of its meaning reached her, and she acted in accordance with its philosophy.

Using her fake illness, Lillian cancelled a class meeting and failed to provide a write-up she'd promised to deliver to the yearbook committee by Wednesday. And she was far too sick to wash the supper dishes or fold the laundry. Her mother looked concerned, and gave her some over-the-counter medication. Lillian took it upstairs and flushed it all down the toilet. Then she returned to her assignment.

The result of all this toil and subterfuge was, of course, a perfect assignment. The facts were accurate and profuse. Data from the text had been puffed out by information from the family's encyclopedia, and from a book on Brazil that her family had won as a bonus from the Book of the Month Club. Her atlas was propped up on the shelf beside her bed, open at page 34: South America. Lillian had painstakingly traced maps and filled in the pertinent parts in pencil crayons and coloured ink. There were neat tables of facts and figures, even a colour picture of the president of Brazil, cut out from a *Life* magazine article called "Presidents of Our Time." Lillian had worked hard, but as she ate her cornflakes and buttered her toast on Thursday morning, she took pleasure in the results of all that appalling effort. She had saved her spot on the basketball team; she'd also made certain that her free afternoons could be put to good use soliciting advertising for the yearbook's back pages, and for preparing the text for a fast-approaching deadline at the printer's. Best of all, the stern, uncompromising Miss Hackett would recognize her as more than just the possessor of a good brain; she'd realize that she was a disciplined and willing worker. Well, *willing* was perhaps not accurate, but she'd *done it,* hadn't she? In any case, she could hardly wait to see the expression of astonishment and delight on Miss Hackett's face. Somewhat to her surprise, Lillian suddenly knew that her work had been more than a crass act of self-preservation, made possible by a bare-faced lie. It had also arisen out of a desire to please.

"Feeling better, dear?" asked her mother. "Do you think you should be going to school?"

"I'm fine," said Lillian, her mouth full of her second slice of toast. "Whatever it was, it's gone."

The radio was offering national and local news. It was the last year of the war and the situation looked good for the Allies.

"Hitler must be getting nervous," said her father from behind the newspaper.

The local news was dull. No murders, no break-ins, no arson. The road report was much as usual. There was congestion on Barrington Street, and cars were moving slowly on Spring Garden Road. A two-car collision was tying up traffic at Quinpool and Robie. Cars were advised to choose an alternative route. The weather report wasn't encouraging. "Rain at times heavy, winds of twenty-five miles per hour, gusting to fifty-five." Lillian took her assignment, tenderly wrapped it in cellophane, and put it in her waterproof swimming bag. The last thing she needed at this point was to have it blow away or be drenched with rain.

Lillian walked to school, head down, bucking the wind, squinting against the onslaught of the driving rain. But she hardly felt the discomfort. She hugged her swimming bag close to her chest, savouring her feeling of triumph and vindication. Not lazy. Not disgusting. A bit of a liar, perhaps, and a breaker of promises, but also a person in charge of her own life. She'd vowed to show that woman, and she'd done it.

Her eyes were on the sidewalk. She didn't notice the crowd of students standing around in the rain.

She failed to see the tow truck or the flashing lights of the police cars. But she now heard the screaming sirens of the ambulances as they raced up the street. Quinpool and Robie. *On* Robie, in fact—not fifty feet from the entrance to the school.

Lillian looked at the cars, transfixed. They were smashed to a degree that she'd seen only in newspaper pictures. Nevertheless, she recognized one of the cars, a light blue Hudson. She watched while two people were carefully manoeuvred out of the wreckage and placed on stretchers—one from each car. She couldn't see the faces, but she saw blood dribbling out of the blue car, mixing with the rain and disappearing. The crowd watched as the ambulances moved away—this time more slowly, more carefully. Lillian walked into the school, eyes wide, staring at nothing, hugging her assignment even more tightly to her chest.

It was early, but the halls seemed to be full of students—talking in quiet, shocked voices, some of them whispering. Lillian walked through the crowds, not stopping to ask questions. But words jumped out at her as she moved along: "… screams … blood … so long to get them out … unconscious … awful," and then, of course, over and over again, "Miss Hackett."

Lillian walked up the stairs to Miss Hackett's homeroom, and stood in the doorway. The room was empty. She realized that Miss Hackett's periods would be taken today by a hastily summoned substitute teacher, or possibly by the principal himself. She knew without being told that Miss Hackett wouldn't return on Thursday, or for weeks or months of Thursdays. The word *never* slid into her mind, and she pushed it out. But it continued to hang in the air of the empty classroom. Carefully, Lillian took the assignment out of the swimming bag, out of the cellophane wrap. Slowly, ceremoniously, she laid the work in the dead centre of Miss Hackett's tidy desk. Like flowers on a hospital bed table, she thought. Or a wreath on a grave.

Lillian is exhausted by these glimpses into this particular compartment of her brain. The images are fuzzy, and she knows that before very long she'll be asleep. But before she drops off, she sees two more scenes out of her past.

She sees herself walking slowly back to Miss Hackett's classroom at the end of the day. She's not sure why. Maybe it's to look once more at her perfect assignment sitting on the exact centre of the desk. Maybe it's to pay a homage of sorts.

But when she looks in the room, Lillian sees that her geography project is no longer where she had so ritualistically placed it. Instead, there is an untidy pile of papers, an attendance sheet, a half-full cup of cold coffee. Over to the left she sees her assignment lying crookedly on top of a bookcase. It no longer looks like a solemn offering. It looks like a discarded envelope.

Quietly, Lillian goes into the room and removes her project from the bookcase. Word had reached the students at lunchtime that Miss Hackett is alive but in a coma.

Lillian will send the assignment and a large get-well card to the hospital. The envelope will be there waiting for her when she awakens. People are saying that she will never regain consciousness. But Lillian knows—without a moment's doubt—that she will wake up. Miss Hackett isn't someone to let a little thing like a coma hold her down.

Lillian enters one more compartment of her brain before she falls asleep. The pictures are very dim, but she sees herself and her husband—in their mid-twenties—backpacking through a tropical country. The going is rough, and there are dangers on all sides—snakes, wild animals, strange food, the possibility of disease. But there are also marvels to behold—great cities, native artifacts, warm-hearted people, spectacular scenery. Lillian hears them speaking Portuguese to the people they meet, and the couple seems to know exactly where they are going and how to get there. "Brazil," murmurs Lillian, as she slips into sleep.

Big Little Jerome

Jerome Seaboyer was always small. He was born in the village of Periwinkle Pond on the South Shore of Nova Scotia, where his father was a fisherman, and where everybody knew something about everybody else. On his arrival, the other mothers gathered around and clucked, "Oh my, oh my! So little. I hope he's okay." They held their own big, sturdy babies smugly, and looked with pity at his mother.

Mrs. Seaboyer, just home from the hospital with her tiny bundle, felt anger rise in her throat and said coolly, "He's fine. He's perfect. He's beautiful." Secretly she thought the other babies fat and lumpy, but she didn't say so. Nor did she admire their eyes or their feet or their gassy smiles. Instead she said, "I'm beginning to feel a bit tired," and held open the front door. The women left, well satisfied with their visit. But thin lines began to form across Mrs. Seaboyer's forehead. She sat down on the bottom step of the stairway, and worried. She worried off and on for the rest of her life.

Even when Jerome started to get older, he kept on being small. He walked by himself at nine months, and Mrs. Rhodenizer said it gave her the creeps to see anything that little walking around. Mrs. Seaboyer took note of the fact that Harrison Rhodenizer was fourteen months old and still couldn't do anything but *sit*. She didn't say so right out. She smiled sweetly at Mrs. Rhodenizer and asked, "Should I push the sharp things to the back of the table so that Harrison can't hurt himself?" knowing full well that she could have put hand grenades on the table without Harrison's being in any danger at all.

When Jerome was finally old enough to go to school, Mrs. Seaboyer waved goodbye as he boarded the school bus for the first time. She wondered how he could possibly survive at school. He looked young enough to be in diapers, and there he was, leaving her sheltering arms for seven hours every day.

Actually, Mrs. Seaboyer could have relaxed. Jerome did just fine. At five and a half years old, he was full of fun and always knew how to make people laugh, even on foggy days and during hurricanes. He was very smart, and he sailed through school with high marks and bright ideas. He was a good swimmer and a quick runner, and he won all the track-and-field ribbons for any event requiring speed. The gym instructor named him "Grease" because, he said, he was like greased lightning. But even when Jerome was in fourth grade, people would stop him on the road, stoop down on a level with his nose, and ask, "Do you go to school yet, little boy?" He used to laugh and say, "Sure! I'm in Grade 4!" and then wait to enjoy their looks of surprise. Jerome was a very happy person.

But this state of affairs could not go on forever. Unlike Jerome, Mrs. Seaboyer could look ahead, and maybe that's why those lines never left the centre of her forehead. She knew that one day Jerome would wake up and realize that when a man gets older, a lot of things are easier and more pleasant if he's tall. Sure enough, the day after his thirteenth birthday, Jerome met Mrs. Rhodenizer in Dorey's Variety Store. She looked down at him and said, "My heavenly days, Jerome! Still so *small!* For goodness' sake, you'll be in high school next year and all the girls will be taller than you. Aren't you *ever* going to get any bigger?"

Jerome felt a cold wind blow across his heart. He didn't know what to say. He looked for a second into her nearsighted eyes; they were peering down at him through glasses so thick that they looked like the bottoms of pop bottles. He felt like an insect stuck on a pin. Then he lowered his gaze roughly in the direction of her belly button. "Maybe so. Maybe no," he chanted lightly. Mrs. Rhodenizer thought his reply was rude, and said so. Of course, Harrison Rhodenizer was more than five foot six already and his voice was starting to change. He also did poorly in school, fell all over his feet, and was as fat as a pudding.

From that moment on, Jerome became a secret worrier. He realized that what Mrs. Rhodenizer had said was absolutely correct. The girls *were* all taller than he was, including Andrea Doucette, the prettiest girl in his class. Andrea sat in front of him at school, and he loved to look at the back of her head and the way the sun shone on her long, straight, blond hair. Sometimes he would just sit there and think up words to describe it: honey, gold, wheat, sunshine, dandelion.

It is true that Andrea seemed to like Jerome. When she was class president, she always chose him first for spelling bees and relay races. But this was elementary school. What about next year? Being short could really begin to matter in high school.

Jerome started locking himself in the bathroom in order to measure his height against the towel rack, and to inspect his face for signs of whiskers. The towel rack stayed in the same place, and so did Jerome. His small handsome face was as smooth as paper. His body was well built and muscular—all four foot six of it. He had thrilling dreams in which he was seven feet tall, his face lost behind a thick, jet-black beard. In these dreams he spent a lot of time saving less gifted swimmers from drowning—people like Harrison Rhodenizer, who couldn't swim a stroke. And night after night he carried Andrea Doucette out of burning buildings, single-handed.

Jerome started to develop lines between *his* eyebrows. Outwardly he was the same as ever: full of jokes, everyone's pal, the life of the party, athletic, smart. But inside, he had sinking feelings. He could visualize a long life ahead of him as an undersized bachelor, reading his books and eating his dinners alone in a pint-sized house, while other men came home to tall, loving wives and enormous families.

Mrs. Seaboyer, who could usually tell exactly what Jerome was thinking, did all she could. She searched for clothes in small sizes that didn't look like kindergarten styles. She fed him masses of vitamins and prayed for growth. She read articles on the mysteries of the pituitary gland. She told him that he looked, and was, marvellous. Jerome admired her strategy, but he saw through it.

His father, for his part, pretended his son was of normal size, and taught him all the fishing lore he knew. Jerome learned about the inshore fisheries, could dress a fish with flair, knew how to recognize the right wood for making lobster traps, and could mend a net and prop up a wharf as well as anybody. He was as prepared for life as it was possible for him to be. But he heard the women whisper when he passed, "A sweet boy! Sad!" And he hated it when the men referred to him as "a nice little feller."

Then his voice changed. It happened gradually, with the usual embarrassing cracks and lurches in his vocal cords. But soon—much sooner than with the other boys—his voice was complete. And it was magnificent. It was deep and rich and powerful. He sang in the bathtub at top volume. He thought up excuses to talk in class. His shouted instructions on the basketball court and at the skating rink were thundering.

But once the first thrill was over, Jerome's vocal talent threw him into further fits of depression. The contrast between what he was and what he was not was so obvious that he felt more ridiculous than he had before. What was this king-sized voice doing coming from a little boy's body? To add to his problems, things kept coming up at school that worried him. Things like the Christmas dance. Jerome knew he would sit at home and watch TV and wish he were dead. He decided to concoct an illness. Twenty-four-hour stomach flu would do. Certainly no girl would want to dance around the gym with *him*.

One Thursday afternoon, Jerome met Andrea Doucette as he was leaving the variety store. They were talking about homework and the usual things, when suddenly Andrea blurted out, "Jerome, would you like to go to the dance with me?" He was stunned. All he could think of to say was, "Oh. Well. Okay. I guess so." Then he turned and left her standing on the steps of the store. In a kind of trance, he walked as far as the breakwater. He stopped then, and stared out at the horizon, full of amazement. Finally he swung around and looked at Andrea. She was staggering under the weight of two bags of groceries, and suddenly they went crashing to the ground. When

Jerome rushed back to help her, he saw tears in her eyes. Picking up the groceries, he asked, "What's the matter? Why are you crying?"

"I'm not, *really*," she said, blinking her eyes. "It's just that I'm shy, and you're popular and athletic, and I'm just me. And all you said was, 'Oh. Well. Okay. I guess so.' It was like you slapped me."

Jerome just looked at her. He looked *up* at her, of course, because she was taller than he was. Then he told her he had been too surprised to say anything. As he carried her groceries home for her, he talked about being short, and how awful it was.

Andrea stopped in her tracks and stared at him. "What do you want, Jerome Seaboyer?" she asked, brown eyes flashing. *Everything?*" Then she looked even fiercer, and went on, "Who do you want to be, if you don't want to be you? Harrison Rhodenizer? Robert MacIntosh? Your father? Ewart Boutilier? Oh, for Pete's sake!"

Suddenly Jerome needed to be alone. He thrust the groceries down on Andrea's porch and muttered, "Gotta go. See you tomorrow." Then he rushed home and picked up his skates, and ran all the way to Little Gull Lake.

The lake was smooth and perfect and untouched. Most people liked to skate on Morrison's Pond, because it was bigger. But here, there was not a mark on the ice. He put on his skates and went out to the rock that broke the surface in the middle of the lake. There he sat down to think. He was in possession of an important thought, and he needed enough quiet to look at all sides of it. *Did* he, as Andrea had suggested, want *everything?* Well, yes, as a matter of fact, he did. He knew he had almost all the things that most people wanted out of life, but he longed for that one special, important, extra thing that would make everything perfect.

Jerome rested his chin on his fist and thought some more. Okay then, did he want to be Harrison Rhodenizer? Poor old, dumb old Harrison Rhodenizer, who had to put up with his nosy mother? No, *thanks.* And Robert MacIntosh? No. He was tall, but he had rotten teeth and his parents drank all the time. His own father, then? A great guy, of course, but *old.* Half of his life was over. He did nothing but work. What about Ewart Boutilier? That was trickier. Andrea must have thrown in that name to make him think. *Really* think. Ewart Boutilier was the tallest boy in the class, handsome, popular, and intelligent. The girls chased after him, or stood around in the halls and giggled when he walked by. He was even *nice*. Jerome thought hard about Ewart. And then, suddenly, he knew. He would like to have *parts* of Ewart—his height, and his fatal charm with the girls. But he did not want to *be* Ewart Boutilier. He, Jerome Seaboyer, wanted to be Jerome Seaboyer. He wanted his own parents, his own special friends, his brains, his sense of humour, his house, his own thoughts and feelings and loves—even his own fears and hates and worries. He wanted to be himself.

Jerome felt as though a ton had been lifted from the back of his neck. He rose from the rock and started to skate, wildly, beautifully, around the lake. He skated in curves and circles, jumping over rocks and spinning around cracks, and then racing at dangerous speeds from one side of the lake to the other. He threw his arms wide, and with his beautiful voice shouted to the trees, "I'm *me*! I'm *me*!" Up above, the sky was blue and cloudless and high. He felt as though he could touch it.

I won't say that Jerome never again minded being short. Of course he did. But the concern ceased to smother him, to poison him. He went to the school dance and decided that dancing was even more fun than basketball. He discovered, over the years, that girls were attracted to him, and when he wanted a girlfriend he could always find one. Later on, he became a strong, skilful, and respected fisherman. He married Andrea Doucette, and they had six children—some short, some tall—and they lived in a big house that he built himself, overlooking the western ledges. He lived to be an old man, full of wit and wonderful stories, beloved of his family and his friends. He never grew to be over five feet tall, and he was a very happy man.

author's note

"Big Little Jerome" was first published in *Crackers* in the Spring issue, 1985. At the time, I was asked to remove the last paragraph, ending the story with the sentence, "He felt as though he could touch it."

Since the story appeared, I have read it aloud to many hundreds of students between the ages of ten and fourteen I always read both endings of the story, and then ask my audience to choose which one they prefer. Typically, out of a class of thirty listeners, two or three want to end it after the second last paragraph. Twenty-seven or twenty-eight opt for the ending you have just read. I then ask the students for the reasons for their choices, because there are a number of very valid defences for choosing either ending. And they have supported their choices well.

But surely the weight of the numbers preferring the latter ending is significant. Do I not, as a writer, have an obligation to listen to what young people want when they read a story? I vowed that if any other publishers asked to use "Big Little Jerome" again, I would tell them exactly how most of the children chose to have that story end.

Since then, it has been published in one collection of short stories and in two anthologies. Each time, I have presented my argument. "Look at the statistics," I've said. "Out of 3,000 students who have heard that story, approximately 250 preferred to end it with the words 'He felt as though he could touch it.' That ending is certainly more subtle, more artistic. But 2,750 preferred the ending that includes the last paragraph." The students have wanted to know that Jerome's acceptance of himself lasted beyond that one afternoon on Little Gull Lake. Then I've said, *"I feel that we need to listen to what the readers are saying."*

Up until now, that plea has been ignored. But Penguin and its editors listened, and have concluded the story with that last paragraph—which contains what I wanted to say, and also, apparently, what most students wanted to hear. For that, I am very grateful. I wonder how the readers of this book will feel about our final choice.

Maid of Honour

Julianna Smith is lying in bed, waiting for the sun to rise. "I want everything to be over so that I can look back on it," she says, picking away at the raised nubbles of her bedspread, chewing the inside of her lip. She's been talking out loud to herself ever since she was three. She's fifteen now, and still doing it. "I'll make a wonderfully well adjusted old person. Everything behind. Nothing ahead."

She flips over briefly, pressing all of herself into the bed. Face, breasts, stomach, knees. Then, sighing, she turns over on her side. Her lips move. "Be with me today," she whispers into the matted fur of her ancient teddy bear. "Let me be able to handle it."

She's not talking to the teddy bear, of course. She's talking to God. And feeling guilty.

Julianna looks around at the part of her room that's visible from this angle. She squashes the bear's head down under the covers so that she can see more. It's not really dark, but it's not very light, either. She fixes her eyes on her Garfield mobile, hanging motionless from the ceiling. *No wind,* she thinks, *so it'll probably be hot.* She's trying to keep her mind off her guilt.

To the left is the window, with the curtains drawn tightly across to keep out the light. "So that I'll sleep a long time," she mutters bitterly, avoiding the luminous dial of her clock, which could tell her that it's five-thirty; but she doesn't want to know. Straight ahead is the Great Big Sea poster and a large picture of Natalie McMaster with her wild blond hair flying; but the light is still too dim to pick up any details. "I wonder if they get nervous before performances." She frowns. "Probably not. Too well adjusted. Not neurotic enough."

Julianna switches to her back position again, and shuts her eyes tight—against wakefulness, against anxiety, against guilt, against this awful day. But she's thinking too hard to go back to sleep, and she's squeezing her eyes so hard that they hurt. "Guilt," she says.

Her mother's face appears against the red-black background of her squeezed eyes. She's saying, "If you don't go to church with us, there's a very good chance of your going straight to hell." By now, church or no church, Julianna figures that's where she's going to wind up, anyway.

The next person she sees on her screen is the Reverend Jackson Grimsby. *Grim is right,* she thinks. He's holding forth from the pulpit, voice deep and compelling, arms gesticulating with a lot of athletic and spiritual grace. He has a new gown, and it's a blazing shade of purple. "Prayer is good," he thunders. "Indeed, let us pray." All heads bow. "Dear Lord," he says, "show us how to pray for the *right things*. Keep us from praying for *ourselves*. Show us that unless we pray for *others,* and for the good of the *whole world,* it can be worse than if we don't pray at all." His first wife died of leukemia when she was twenty-eight. Didn't he at least give it a try? Didn't he—even *once*—ask God to save her?

The image fades, and Julianna amends her prayer. "Be with all of us today," she whispers. "Let every one of us be able to handle it." She guesses it's okay to include herself with the whole world, and besides, it's not as though she's praying for an A in geometry or a diamond necklace—neither one of which is apt to happen without the assistance of someone almost as powerful as God.

It's getting lighter. Sunshine is creeping around the edges of the curtains. Julianna can see the longish straight mane of Alan Doyle flipping around as he pounds at his guitar. A great poster. And in the other picture, she can make out the blondness of Natalie's flyaway hair. She dares to look at the clock. It's six-thirty, and she can hear things starting to happen in the kitchen—water running, the slam of the fridge door. And none too soon, either. In exactly eight hours, Julianna will be walking down the aisle of St. Mark's Church. She will be walking alone, with no one to hold her up, at the head of a procession that will include three other bridesmaids, a gaggle of ushers, a flower girl, and finally, her twenty-three-year-old, stunningly confident and gorgeous sister, carelessly holding the arm of their proud father. For five months he's been making a lot of fuss about the cost of the wedding, but as he glides up the aisle with Eileen on his arm, he won't be thinking about money. He'll be thinking that his beautiful and favourite daughter is having the most spectacular wedding ever to be staged along this stretch of the Annapolis Valley. If he concentrates on money at all, it will be to conclude that this wedding has been worth every penny.

That's what he'll be thinking, unless Julianna falls flat on her face as she navigates the church's heat register, strategically situated halfway down the agonizingly long aisle. They'll all be wearing full-length dresses—great for someone like Queen Elizabeth I, or even Jane Eyre. Not so great for Julianna, who spends her life in jeans. And they're all going to be wearing dainty little mauve shoes, dyed especially for the occasion, with *very high heels*. Julianna has practised and practised walking on them, wobbling from one side of the bedroom to the other—practising until her insteps feel as though they're shot through with hot knives. And never once, not even *once,* has she travelled the distance between the door and the window without those skinny little heels wiggling as if they were alive. Furthermore, everyone in the world knows that the hems of long dresses are for tripping over. She has visualized it a thousand times. She's lying flat on her stomach on the register, while the whole wedding procession comes to a dead halt. Or, in other versions of the scenario, the others are all bunched up behind her, staggering and bumping into one another, her father's face a deep and dangerous red, her sister's white with rage. As the wedding party careens and thumps around, the little nosegays tied to the pews will come loose and fall to the ground, thereby providing something else to trip over.

When some people fall or faint, they end up looking like one of the fragile maidens of King Arthur's Court, or like some doomed and delicate victim of nineteenth-century consumption—at her most beautiful as death draws near.

Not Julianna. A farmer once told her she was "a fine, healthy chunk of a girl." Thinking it was a compliment. Sprawled face-down on the register, she's not going to be a lovely sight. While Eileen of the twenty-one-inch waist and flawless skin looks on, her eyes steely blue and unforgiving.

As Julianna pads off to the bathroom for a quick shower, she doesn't give her mind a rest. No. She's still thinking. Last night at the rehearsal, it was fine. It wasn't a *dress* rehearsal, so she didn't have to cope with the long dress or the high heels. And she was so busy looking at Lance O'Neil, the groom's first cousin from New Hampshire, that she forgot she was nervous. She does remember saying, "Please, God," as she started down the aisle, and then she just sauntered along as if it was any old day. But when she looked at Reverend Jackson Grimsby as he issued instructions to the bride and groom, she realized that she'd been praying for herself again. It was almost enough to keep her mind off Lance O'Neil's American accent and his long legs and his wonderfully crooked smile. While all she has going for her is a pair of large green eyes (with a lot of long lashes) and naturally curly hair. Not to mention the guilt that she carries around with her because of saying the wrong things to God all the time. "But *please,* God," she pleads, as she steps out of the shower, "Just this once. Okay?"

It doesn't take Julianna long to realize that everyone in the family is nervous. It's Saturday, so her father isn't at work. He's pacing around, looking as though he doesn't belong in his own house. Julianna guesses he thinks it would be indecent to watch TV or work on the broken lawn mower or fix the can opener, on his special daughter's wedding day. So all he manages to do is get in the way. His wife, always quick moving, is going about her business with accelerated speed. She's triple-checking with the flower shop, the Legion hall, the hairdresser, the taxi company. She keeps administering little pats to Eileen's back or shoulders or cheek whenever she's nearby, muttering things like "It'll all go fine, dear," or "You'll remember this day forever, sweetheart." Eileen is wandering around the house with an irritating air of self-confidence, but when she picks up her coffee mug from the kitchen table, Julianna can see that her hand is shaking.

It's a relief when her mother and Eileen go off to the Sally-Jean Beauty Parlour to have their hair done. Nobody has thought to ask Julianna if she'd like to have something unusual and amazing done to her hair. People with naturally curly hair aren't supposed to want anything like that. In fact, the family is acting pretty much as though Julianna doesn't live here, and although marginally insulted, she's pleased about this. She's so strung out that she's afraid if someone were to say the wrong thing to her at the wrong moment, she might just possibly start to scream, or maybe even slap someone. Guiltily, frantically, she tries approaching God again. "Please," she says, behind the locked bathroom door, "don't let me wreck this wedding." Maybe that's okay. She hopes it will occur to God that she's praying for the whole family and not just *her*. But secretly, under about six layers of subterfuge, she knows that what she's really asking for is her own deliverance from humiliation on the heat register.

It's getting hotter inside, so Julianna goes into her room and closes the door, strips down to her T-shirt and panties, and lies on the bed. She stares at the light fixture, and thinks about how she's trying to fool God into believing she's praying for everyone else, when she really has something entirely different in mind. She couldn't feel more alone.

Suddenly it's one o'clock, and the family is in high gear. Within one hour and fifteen minutes, everyone has to be in those newly polished taxis, driving the six blocks to St. Mark's Church. There's a lot of traffic in the bathroom, and everyone is getting dressed up in unaccustomed formal finery. The father of the bride is having difficulties with his bow tie, but there's no one available to help him. Possibly it occurs to him that the person who is paying for this wedding deserves at least a little assistance. The bridesmaids are all there, fussing over Eileen's minuscule train, her veil, her hairdo—which is threatening to collapse. Mrs. Smith is already dressed in her ankle-length rose-coloured gown, and is dispensing bobby pins and Scotch tape and thread, as needed. She's trying to appear calm, but she's not succeeding, and Julianna sees her popping some kind of yellow pill when she passes the kitchen door. As maid of honour, Julianna supposes that she should be hovering over Eileen, administering nail polish or comfort. But there's no room in Eileen's bedroom for a fifth person. Besides, it's all Julianna can do to keep her own self from flying apart at the seams. So she goes in her room and gets dressed in her full-length mauve dress and her high-heeled mauve shoes. With trembling hands, she puts on her makeup and affixes the circlet of fake violets to her naturally curly hair. Then she sits on the edge of the bed and tries to practise deep breathing without hyperventilating. "*Please,* God," she whispers, between breaths.

It's two o'clock, and everyone knows that the shiny black taxis will come rolling up to the door in ten or fifteen minutes. Julianna decides that she'll wait on the veranda, because she can't stand being in that house any longer—with the squeals of the bridesmaids, the chaos in the kitchen, her father's pacing, the air of dithering crisis. Even if it's too hot outside, she needs to be there. She opens the door, and the day presents itself to her. To begin with, it's not hot. But the sun is picking up every beautiful thing that she's looking at—the Wilkinsons' lilac tree; the apple blossoms in her own front yard; the little red gardening shed that Mr. Hoskins painted last week; the fresh, bright, new green grass; the pink doll carriage that little Millicent McGuire is pushing up and down the street; the glowing brown skin of Mr. Carvery, their neighbour, as he mows the grass with his sleeves rolled up; the multicoloured towels on Mrs. Joggins's clothesline. To Julianna's surprise, she sees that her mother is standing on the far end of the veranda, looking either resigned or calm. She's also smiling.

"No room for me in there," she says. "So I came out here to gather myself together."

These are the first words that Mrs. Smith has spoken to Julianna since the day began.

"Hi, Mom, " says Julianna. "How's it going?"

Mrs. Smith waves her arm around to include the whole scene. "Just look at it!" she exclaims in a voice that is not quite steady. "A truly perfect day. Not too hot. No wind to wreck our hairdos. No rain to drench our dresses." She closes her eyes for a moment. Then she says, "All my prayers have been answered."

Julianna's head snaps around to face her mother. "Your *what?*" she says.

"My prayers," says her mother, with a little laugh. "My specific, detailed wedding prayers."

Julianna speaks slowly. "And what exactly did you pray for?"

Her mother grins. "For a fine day. For the flowers to arrive on time. For zero wind, in order to preserve my hair, which can look like a scarecrow's if the weather is wet or wild. For Eileen not to get hysterical at the last minute. For your father to stop talking about how much it's all costing. For me to be able to pull it all together. And not to throw up in the middle of the vows."

Julianna is speechless. She stares at her mother, who is still talking.

"An elderly nun used to teach me piano lessons. She said that God has two answers to prayers. One is Yes. The other is No. Apparently we got a full-bodied Yes today."

Julianna is finally able to speak. "But Mr. Grimsby says we should only pray for other people. That anything else is wicked."

Mrs. Smith laughs. "Well," she says, "Mr. Grimsby doesn't necessarily know every single thing about God. For one thing, he makes Him sound pretty cold and distant. Besides, what makes him so sure He's a *man*?"

Well, Julianna isn't ready to apply her mind to such a thought. That yellow pill may be doing some pretty funny things to her mother. However, she says, "But a while back, you yourself said that if I didn't go to church with you I'd go straight to hell. What kind of a God would permit *that*?"

Mrs. Smith looks stricken. "Oh, Julianna!" she says. "You didn't really think I *meant* that, did you? It was just a little *joke*. It was Easter Sunday, and I wanted us all to be together. I just threw that in to jolt you out of the TV show you were watching."

The voices inside the house are getting louder, and way down Main Street, four blocks away, Julianna can see the approach of the taxis, fresh from the car wash and moving slowly.

"Just before the others come out," says Mrs. Smith, close to her ear, "I want you to know that I'm sort of looking forward to our time together after Eileen is gone. I love her a lot, of course—a *whole* lot—but she's pretty demanding. It often seems like I haven't had time to enjoy anyone else. She was always *there,* either needing or dictating something, from the moment she was born. But you've seemed to be at home in your own shoes right from the start, able to cope with just about anything." Then she adds, "I'd love to be like you."

The bridesmaids emerge from the house, suddenly quiet and serious. The giggly part is over. Eileen steps onto the veranda, clutching her father's arm, looking both beautiful and terrified. Mr. Smith is acting protective and kind, and it's obvious that he's already forgotten about his depleted bank account. The taxis draw up to the curb. Holding her long skirt, Julianna sails down the steps, ahead of everyone.

In the taxi, and later at the church while they wait for the last guests to arrive, Julianna is alone with her own thoughts. Mr. Grimsby: not infallible. Hell: just a little joke. God: ready to listen to small stuff, possibly even equipped with a sense of humour. Herself: at home in her own shoes, even high-heeled ones. Inside her head, she keeps repeating the words: "I'd love to be like you."

Julianna hears the first evocative chords of the wedding march, and moves across the vestibule to take her place at the head of the procession. She can see the heat register in the middle of the aisle, but she gives it only a superficial glance. When she passes Lance O'Neil as they move into their various positions, he winks at her. She winks back. She knows that her little crown of fake violets looks pretty on her naturally curly hair. And she grins, because by now she's convinced that God is definitely equipped with a sense of humour. "Thanks," she whispers. "Thanks, God."

Then they all move slowly down the church aisle toward the Reverend Jackson Grimsby, toward the groom, and toward Julianna's mother, Mrs. Smith, who is clutching the side of the pew as she watches the procession, with a river of tears streaming down her radiantly happy face.